Praise for
IF I WAS *your* GIRL

"*If I Was Your Girl* is important and necessary and brave, and deeply, electrically inspiring. We should all walk in Amanda's shoes, whether we think we can relate to her or not. Because who can't relate to a story about having the courage to be the person you were meant to be?"
Jennifer Niven, New York Times bestselling author of
All the Bright Places

"*If I Was Your Girl* is real and raw and layered and wonderful."
Alex Gino, author of *George*

"This book will change minds and open hearts."
Nina Lacour, author of *Everything Leads to You*

"A coming-of-age with real world gravitas and a love story with heart. Will not only keep readers hooked, it will make the world a better, more empathetic place."
Adi Alsaid, author of *Let's Get Lost*

"Meredith Russo's debut is poignant and rare. *If I Was Your Girl* is the type of book you read and want to immediately share, because it's too ~~important to keep~~ to yourself."
Jul~~ia~~ ~~bestselling~~ author

First published in the UK in 2016 by Usborne Publishing Ltd., Usborne House, 83-85 Saffron Hill, London EC1N 8RT, England. www.usborne.com. Published by arrangement with Rights People, London.

The name Usborne and the devices ♀⊕ are Trade Marks of Usborne Publishing Ltd.

If I Was Your Girl © 2016 by Alloy Entertainment

alloyentertainment

Produced by Alloy Entertainment, LLC.

A CIP catalogue record for this book is available from the British Library.

ISBN 9781474923835 JFMAM JASOND/16 04235/04.

Printed in the UK.

IF I WAS your GIRL

MEREDITH RUSSO

USBORNE

*For Vivian and Darwin, for giving me the honour
of being a mother.*

*For Juniper, who inspired so much of this book with
her stories and who pushed me when I thought
I couldn't keep going.*

*For my parents, for not flipping out when I majored in writing
(with a minor in women's studies to boot).*

*For all my foremothers and forefathers and those in-between, for
rioting and fighting and surviving plagues and mourning friends,
for coming through pain I can't even imagine to
give me the opportunities and freedoms I have now.*

*For my brothers and sisters and those in-between, for surviving
out there every day and being beautiful inside and out in a
world that's still so far from safe.*

*For the boys and girls and those in-between who feel alone
and afraid, who feel like there's no way out, who feel like things
can never be better than they are now.*

*For all those who didn't make it, who now rest in power
and whose names we will never forget.*

This book is for all of you.

CHAPTER ONE

The bus smelled of mildew, machine oil and sweat. As the suburban Atlanta sprawl disappeared behind us, I tapped my foot on the floor and chewed a lock of my newly long hair. A nagging voice reminded me that I was only a half-hour from home, that if I got off at the next stop and walked back to Smyrna, by sunset I could be in the comfort of my own bedroom, the familiar smell of Mom's starchy cooking in the air. She would hug me and we would sit down and watch awful reality TV shows together and she would fall asleep halfway through, and then nothing would change.

But something had to change. Because I had changed.

As I stared out at the swiftly moving trees, my mind was in a mall bathroom back in the city, the images shifting and jumbling like a kaleidoscope: a girl from my school, her scream as she recognized me. Her father rushing in, his rough, swift hands on my neck and shoulders. My body hitting the ground.

"You okay?" a voice practically screamed in my ear. I looked up to see a guy wearing earbuds, his chin resting on the back of the seat in front of me. He gave me a lopsided smile as he pulled out the headphones. "Sorry."

"It's fine," I said. He stared at me, drumming his fingers on the headrest. I felt like I should say something, but I didn't trust my voice not to give me away.

"Where you headed?" He draped himself across the back of his seat like a cat, his arms nearly grazing my shins. I wished I could roll up into a tiny, armoured ball and hide in my luggage.

"Lambertville," I said quietly. "Up in Hecate County."

"I'm going to Knoxville," he said, before going on to talk about his band, Gnosis Crank. I realized he'd only asked about me as a formality so he could talk about himself, but I didn't mind; it meant I didn't have to say that much. He told me about playing their first paying gig at a bar in Five Points.

"Cool," I said.

"Most of our songs are online if you wanna check them out."

"I will."

"How'd you get that black eye, by the way?"

"I—"

"Was it your boyfriend?" he asked.

My cheeks burned. He scratched his chin. He assumed I had a boyfriend. He assumed I was a girl. Under different circumstances, that would have thrilled me.

"I fell down," I said.

His smile turned sad.

"That's what my mom used to tell the neighbours," he said. "She deserved better, and so do you."

"Okay," I said, nodding. Maybe he was right, but what I deserved and what I could expect from life were two different things. "Thank you."

"No problem," he said as he put his headphones back in. He smiled and added, "Nice meeting you," way too loudly before returning to his seat.

As we headed north on I-75 I texted Mom, letting her know I was okay and halfway there. She wrote back that she loved me, though I could feel her worry through the phone. I imagined her in our house all alone, Carrie Underwood playing on loop while the ceiling fans whispered overhead. Her hands covered in flour folded on the table in front of her, too many biscuits in the oven because she was used to cooking for two. If I'd had the strength to be normal, I thought, or at least the strength to die, then everyone would have been happy.

"Next stop Lambertville," the bus driver called over the harsh, tinny intercom. Outside the windows, none of the scenery had changed. The mountains looked the same. The trees looked the same. We could have been anywhere in the South, which is to say, nowhere. It seemed like the sort of place where Dad would live.

My hands shook as the bus lurched to a stop. I was the only passenger who stood up. The musician looked up from his magazine and nodded while I gathered my things. An older man with leathery skin and a sweat-stained work shirt scanned me from my feet to my neck without making eye contact. I stared straight ahead and pretended not to notice.

The door rattled open and the bus let out a hiss. I closed my eyes, whispered a short prayer to a god I wasn't sure really listened any more, and stepped down. The sickly humid afternoon heat hit me like a solid wall.

It had been six years since I had seen my father. I had rehearsed this moment over and over in my head. I would run up and hug him, and he would kiss the top of my head, and for the first time in a long time, I would feel safe.

"That you?" Dad asked, his voice muffled by the bass rumble of the bus engine. I squinted against the harsh light. He wore a pair of wire-rim sunglasses, and his hair was at least half silver now. Deep lines had formed around his mouth. Mom called these "laugh lines", so I wasn't sure how he had got them. Only his mouth was as I remembered it: the same thin, horizontal slash.

"Hi, Dad," I said. The sunglasses made it easier to look him in the face. We both stood rooted in place.

"Hi," he said after a while. "Put your things in the back." He opened the back of the wagon and got in the car. I deposited my luggage and joined him. I remembered this car; it was at least ten years old, but Dad was good with machines. "You must be hungry."

"Not really," I said. I hadn't been hungry in a while. I hadn't cried in a while. Mostly I just felt numb.

"You should eat." He glanced at me as he pulled out of the parking lot. His lenses had become transparent, and behind them, his eyes were a flat, almost greyish brown. "There's a diner close to the apartment. If we get there now we'll have the place to ourselves."

"That's nice." Dad had never been social, but a little voice in my head said he didn't want to be seen with me. I took a deep breath. "Your glasses are cool."

"Oh?" He shrugged. "Astigmatism got worse. These help."

"It's good that you got it treated," I said, my words as staggered and awkward as I felt. I looked down at my lap.

"You've got my eyes, you know. You should take care of yourself."

"Yes, sir."

"We'll take you to the optometrist soon. Need to get your eye looked at after that shiner anyway."

"Yes, sir." A billboard rose from the trees to the left, depicting a cartoon soldier firing red, white and blue sparks from a bazooka. GENERAL BLAMMO'S FIREWORK

11

SHACK. We turned into the sun so his eyes were hidden again, his jaw set in a way I didn't know how to read. "What did Mom tell you?"

"She was worried about you," he said. "She said you weren't safe where you were living."

"Did she tell you about what happened sophomore year? When I...was in the hospital?"

His knuckles whitened on the steering wheel. He stared ahead silently as we passed an old brick building with a tarnished steeple. The sign read NEW HOPE BAPTIST CHURCH. A Walmart loomed behind it.

"We can talk about that later." He adjusted his glasses and sighed. The lines in his skin seemed to deepen. I wondered how he had aged so much in six years, but then I remembered how much I had changed too.

"Sorry," I said. "I shouldn't have brought it up." I watched the patchwork tobacco farms roll by. "It's just, you never called or wrote."

"Wasn't sure what I could say," he said. "It's been hard coming to terms with...everything."

"Have you come to terms now that you've seen me?"

"Give me time, kiddo." His lips puckered as they formed the last word, so unusually informal for him. "I guess I'm just old-fashioned."

The turn signal clicked in time with my heart as the car slowed. We pulled up in front of the Sartoris Diner Car, an actual converted railroad car on a cinder-block foundation.

"I understand," I said. I imagined how I must look to him, and my mind leaped to fill in all the worst things I had ever felt about myself. "My name is Amanda now though, in case you forgot."

"Okay," he said. He killed the engine, opened the door, and hesitated. "Okay, Amanda. I can do that." He walked to the front door in that clockwork way of his, hands in his pockets and elbows pointed at symmetrical angles. I couldn't help seeing my reflection in the window: a gangly teenage girl with long, brown hair in a cotton shirt and shorts rumpled from travel.

A bell jingled as we entered the empty diner. A sleepy-eyed waitress looked up and smiled. "Hi, Mr Hardy!"

"Afternoon, Mary Anne," he said, grinning broadly and waving as he took a seat at the counter. That smile gave me a feeling of vertigo. He had smiled when I was seven and I told him I wanted to try out for Little League. He had smiled when I was nine and I agreed to go hunting with him. I couldn't remember any other times. "Heard your granny had a stroke. How y'all holding up?"

"She says heaven don't want her and hell's afraid she'd take over," the girl said, pulling a notebook and pen from her apron and walking over. "The physical therapy's been a bear, though."

"She can do it if anybody can," Dad said. He slid his menu to her without looking at it. "Sweet tea and a Caesar salad with chicken, please."

She nodded. "And who's this with you?" she asked, turning to me. My eyes flicked from her to Dad.

"I'm Amanda," I said. She looked like she expected more information, but I had no idea what Dad had told people about his family. What if he told them he had one child, a son? I shakily handed her my menu and said, "I would like a waffle and Diet Coke, please, ma'am, thank you."

"She's my daughter," Dad said after a moment, his voice halting and stiff.

"Well, she looks just like you!" We exchanged an uncomfortable look as Mary Anne trotted off to get our drinks.

"She seems nice," I said.

"She's a good waitress," Dad said. He nodded stiffly. I drummed my fingers on the counter and wiggled my foot back and forth absent-mindedly.

"Thank you for letting me stay with you," I said softly. "It means a lot."

"Least I could do."

Mary Anne brought our food and excused herself to greet a pair of white-haired older men in plaid work shirts.

One of the men stopped to talk to Dad. His nose was round and spiderwebbed with purple veins, his eyes hidden under storm-cloud brows. "Who's this little beam of sunshine?" he asked, leaning past Dad to wave at me. I turned so he couldn't see my black eye.

"Amanda," Dad mumbled. "My daughter."

The man whistled and slapped Dad's shoulder. "Well, no wonder I ain't seen her before! If I had a daughter as cute as this'n I'd keep her hid away too." My cheeks burned. "You just tell me if any of the boys get too fresh, now, and I'll loan you my rifle."

"I don't think that will be a problem," Dad said haltingly.

"Oh, trust me," he said, winking, "I had three daughters, not a one of them half as pretty as this one in their time, and it was still all I could do to keep the boys away."

"Okay," Dad said. "Thanks for the advice. Looks like your coffee's getting cold."

The man said goodbye, winked again, and walked stiffly to his seat. I turned my attention straight ahead. Out of the corner of my eye I noticed Dad doing the same.

"Ready to go?" he asked finally.

He got up without waiting for a response and threw a twenty-dollar bill on the table next to our half-finished meals. We didn't make eye contact as we got in the car and pulled out of the parking lot.

NOVEMBER, THREE YEARS AGO

The hospital bed creaked as Mom sat and rubbed my leg through the thin blanket. A forced smile tightened her apple cheeks but failed to reach her eyes. Her clothes looked baggy; she must not have eaten since I was admitted, to have lost so much weight.

"I talked with the counsellor," she said. Her accent was so different from mine, light and musical.

I said, "What about?" My voice sounded like nothing – flat, toneless, with the faintest deepening that made me never want to speak again. My stomach cramped and twisted.

"When it's safe for you to come home. I told 'em I was worried 'bout what you might do when you're alone, since I can't take any more time off work. I couldn't survive it if I came home and found you…" She trailed off, staring at the light-yellow wall.

"What did the counsellor say?" I had met with him a few days before. When he asked me what was wrong with me, I wrote six words on a notepad, my throat still too sore from the stomach pump to speak.

"He said there's ways to treat what's wrong with you," Mom said. "But he wouldn't say what it is." She peered at me.

"You won't want me to come home if I tell you what's wrong," I said, shifting my eyes down. "You won't ever want to see me again." This was the most I'd said at once in weeks. My throat ached from the effort.

"That ain't possible," she said. "There ain't a thing in God's creation that could undo the love I have for my son."

I brought my wrist up to my chest and looked down. The identification bracelet said my name was Andrew Hardy. If I died, I realized, Andrew was the name they would put on my tombstone.

"What if your son told you he was your daughter?"

My mother was quiet for a moment. I thought of the words I wrote down for the counsellor: *I should have been a girl.*

Finally, she brought her eyes to meet mine. Her expression was fierce, despite her round, red cheeks.

"Listen to me." Her hand squeezed my leg hard enough that the pain broke through the fog of my meds. When she spoke next, I listened. "Anything, *anyone*, is better than a dead son."

CHAPTER TWO

Lambertville High sat at the bottom of a hill, dozens of beat-up trucks and station wagons clustered near the entrance. Small pockets of students hovered near the front door, the boys conspicuously slouched and the girls straight-backed and high-chinned, all radiating as much transparent disinterest in one another as possible.

I had barely slept the night before. I gave up trying at five and drank a chocolate-flavoured nutritional shake with my medicine: two two-milligram estradiol tablets, which were tiny and blue and tasted like chalk, to feminize my appearance and stand in for the testosterone my body could no longer make, and one ten-milligram Lexapro tablet, which was round and white and waxy, to help me stay calm.

I kept my eyes straight ahead and walked through the double doors, hoping the concealer I wore over the faded, yellowish remnants of my black eye did its job. Inside, the floor was an alternating pattern of green, brown and gold-flecked white tiles. Fluorescent lights buzzed angrily, but for all their fury, the halls were dimly lit. Display cases lined the walls, shelf after shelf of trophies for cheerleading, marching band, baseball, and especially football, with records reaching back far enough that half the team photos were sepia-toned. The red classroom doors bore faded-looking numbers, and I followed them to 118, the homeroom marked on my schedule.

More than a dozen students sat in groups of three or four, talking so loudly I could hear them in the hall. The room fell quiet as I entered. The girls looked at me and then away again quickly, but a few guys stared for a second longer, their expressions unreadable.

As I moved to find a seat, one face was still turned my way: a tall, lean boy with dark, sharp eyes and wavy black hair. Our eyes caught, and I felt a lurch in my stomach. He sat with another boy, this one tall and bulky with short light hair and a nose that looked like it had been broken before, a half-lidded, sarcastic expression pointed at me. The sarcastic-looking one said something I couldn't make out, and a crimson blush spread across his friend's cheeks.

My heart screamed that they knew, that the one with those piercing eyes was attracted to me for a moment and his friend was making fun of him for it. That was the kind of scenario that got girls like me killed. I had done the research. I knew how often things like that happened. I felt the scar over my ear and remembered that even now that I'd had my surgery, even now that nothing but some legal papers could reveal my past, I was never really safe.

I looked down at my lap and tried to will myself out of existence.

The cafeteria and the auditorium were the same room. The tables were circular, each seating at most five or six people, and half of the seating was on the stage itself. The higher position was clearly reserved for juniors and seniors.

I sat at an empty table on the stage and opened up *Sandman*, a comic book my friend Virginia had recommended, and pulled out the vegetable sushi rolls I had prepared the night before. After a few minutes, I marked my place and ducked to put the book away – and looked up to find the black-haired boy from homeroom sitting across from me.

"Hi," he said. He wasn't as tall or bulky as his friend, but the muscles in his arms were lean, and he moved with a relaxed grace. "Mind if I sit here?"

"Yes," I said, realizing too late that I was being rude. "I'm fine, I mean."

"My friend Parker thinks so," he replied.

"Excuse me?" I said, nearly choking on a glob of wasabi. "Sorry," I coughed, before taking a sip of water. "Spicy."

"Where'd you get sushi in Lambertville?" he asked, pointing to what was left of my lunch.

"I made it," I said, nervously fiddling with my chopsticks.

"Wow," he said. "I didn't know you could just... *make* sushi."

"It's not that hard," I lied, remembering the countless nights I had spent at my mom's kitchen table, trying to get the rice to stick together. When the stress of transitioning had become too much, my doctors insisted I take some time off. The year at home had seemed fun at first, like an extended summer break, but eventually boredom kicked in. I had started to feel like I was just standing still, like life was passing me by outside and I would be forever trapped in our house with nowhere to go and no one to talk to. I had to occupy myself somehow.

He looked surprised. "Most families around here think a fancy meal is getting Italian instead of Tex-Mex. And I'm Grant, if you were wondering."

"Okay," I said. The back of my neck tingled. "I'm Amanda."

"Sorry for choking you with my lame pun, Amanda," he said. "I meant it as a compliment, but that kind of thing must be pretty old at this point."

"Why would you say that?"

"A girl like you?"

I narrowed my eyes. What did he mean, *a girl like me*?

21

My fears from earlier returned in a rush. "Are you messing with me?"

"You're just fishing for more compliments now," he said, shaking his head and laughing. "Fine, whatever. Did you see the dude with the nose situation who sat by me in homeroom?" I nodded slowly and swallowed. "That's my friend Parker. He wants to ask you out, but he's a big chickenshit, so here I am asking for your number for him."

"You want my number?" I put my hands in my lap. Blood pounded in my temples. People who looked like Grant had never spoken to me without secretly planning to hurt me. For so many years I'd been on the wrong side of too many jokes, too many pranks, too many confrontations. I'd been knocked down a hundred times in a hundred different ways. "For your friend."

"Yup," he said.

"My dad's, um, really strict," I said. I thought of the look on his face at the diner when the old man had offered to lend him a rifle to use on my suitors. It wasn't entirely a lie. He furrowed his brow and leaned forward on his elbows. For some reason, I felt compelled to go on. "It's complicated...I'm complicated." I pursed my lips tight and felt my nostrils flare. I was saying too much.

"Okay," Grant said easily, leaning back in his chair. A moment of taut silence followed as those charcoal eyes flickered over my face. In them I saw curiosity, but not menace. I wondered if a boy like him could ever understand

22

what it was like to be me. To know what it was like to view high school as something you needed to survive. Because that was all it was to me, a series of days to get through, boxes on a calendar to be crossed off. I had come to Lambertville with a plan: I would keep my head down and keep quiet. I would graduate. I would go to college as far from the South as I could. I would live.

"For the record –" Grant rubbed the back of his neck – "I told Parker this would go better if he came by himself. But he's my buddy, you know? So I had to try. He's a horse's ass, though, and you probably think I am too now. "

"I don't," I said. I started to put my things away and realized my hands were shaking. I believed he was earnest, or at least I wanted to, but my fear had been carved into me over years and years, and it wasn't going to be reasoned with or ignored. "It would have gone the same way if he'd come himself. I – I just can't."

A look crossed Grant's face I couldn't quite read. He slipped his hands in his pockets and stood. "Well, it was very nice meeting you, Amanda."

"You too," I said. My cheeks felt warm.

Grant gave me a small wave and walked away. He stopped after a few steps and turned.

"What book is that?" he said, nodding to the table.

"*Sandman,*" I said, putting a hand over it protectively. "It's a comic book."

"Is it good?"

23

"I think so," I said.

"Cool," Grant said, waving again and turning to leave. My hands stopped shaking and my breathing slowed, but for some reason I was afraid to consider, my heart wouldn't stop racing in my chest.

CHAPTER
THREE

Art class came last on Mondays and Tuesdays, and was in the music building at the edge of the school grounds. Outside, the withering heat hit me swiftly, my skin like shrink-wrap under a blow dryer.

"Around back," a female voice called as I reached the shed-sized wooden building. I followed it, finding a girl alone in the grass. Oval sunglasses shielded her eyes and bright-red lipstick contrasted with her pale skin. Dark bristles grew on a third of her head while the other two-thirds sported a thick, wavy halo of hair.

"Art class?" she said. I nodded and looked around uneasily. She propped herself up on her elbows. "Teacher's in Nashville. Her son fucked up his hand in a car accident."

"Oh God."

"Right? He's a musician too. Was a musician. Hey, it's hot as shit out here and you look like you're about to have a heart attack. Why don't you sit? Name's Bee, by the way."

"Shouldn't we go to the office?"

"Jesus, no," she said quickly. "They won't hire a sub. They won't hire a new teacher. They'll put my fat ass in PE and move all the art funding to the athletic department like they do with everything. I'm gonna milk this shit for everything it's worth."

I nodded weakly and sat. The girl flopped back down with her arms spread wide.

"So you're the new girl?"

"That obvious?" I said, pulling my knees close.

"Word gets around." Sweat glistened on her arms and legs, her face pointed up at the sky.

"Oh, right. Sorry."

"You don't have to apologize," she said, still barely moving.

"Sorry," I said reflexively, then winced.

"You know you never told me your name, right?"

"Amanda," I said quickly. "Nice to meet you."

"Sure." She fished in her battered old Silver Age X-Men lunch box and pulled out a joint. "Mind if I smoke?" She didn't wait for an answer.

"So," she said, blowing out a smoky speech bubble. The smell was like mulch after a heavy rainstorm, earthy and a little sour. "Where you from?"

"Smyrna," I told her. "Dad moved here after the divorce."

"Dads," she observed. I didn't have a response, but she either didn't notice or didn't care. "You're pretty cool, Amanda. I think we're gonna be friends."

"I don't know how cool I am," I said.

"We'll see," Bee said, nodding as she put the half-smoked joint back in the lunch box. "Oh, we will see." She giggled and lay back in the grass, closing her eyes.

I fell back beside her and started to read *Sandman*, holding the book up above me to shield my eyes from the sun. I was quickly caught up in the story. As people all around the world fell asleep and never awakened again, I lost track of time. The Lord of Dreams managed to escape after decades of imprisonment to try to rebuild his life. The sleepers woke up to find themselves in bodies they didn't recognize, subject to the consequences of abuse while they were helpless. Finally, as the Lord of Dreams descended into hell, I put the book away.

Sitting up, the afternoon heat seemed to pulse and throb. I glanced over at Bee, who was in a sort of trance, half-asleep, half-awake. "What's the time, anyway?"

"Four," she said as she yawned and flopped back onto the grass.

"Shit," I said, scrambling to jam my notebook in my bag. I heard the buses hiss into motion as I stood up and ran around the corner to find a mostly empty parking lot.

"Miss your ride? Shitty," Bee said. "Anybody you can call?"

"Dad doesn't get off until six."

"I'd give you a ride," she said, "but I don't drive stoned, which is super, super what I am right now. Stoned like a witch in Salem…" She snickered dreamily at her joke.

"I have to walk then," I said.

"I wouldn't," Bee said in a sing-song voice. "High's 113 today. Heatstroke territory."

"Teenagers don't get heatstroke though, right? I mean, logically, people lived in the South for a long time before air-conditioning."

"Your funeral," she said with a lazy wave. "See you around if you don't die."

Sweat poured down my back as I walked along the shoulder of the road. After the first thirty minutes I had covered two of the six miles, but I panted and dragged my feet. I thought about calling Dad, but didn't want to bother him on my very first day. I made it another mile, but my knees ached and my bare calves stung, scratched up from the brambles. My tongue felt dry, and my head throbbed.

I barely registered as a black car blasted by, then reversed to a stop on the shoulder beside me.

The window rolled down and a pale girl with short dark hair leaned out. "Need a ride?"

"Nah," I slurred, "I don't wanna trouble anybody."

She turned to someone in the back seat. "I don't care what she said, Chloe, just get her in here before she passes out."

A girl with a curly red mane and freckles appeared, squinting painfully in the bright light. She wore a chequered work shirt unbuttoned at mid-chest and rolled up at the sleeves. Without saying a word she took me by the arm and walked me to the rear left seat.

"Really, it's okay…" I said weakly, but I closed my eyes as the cold air-conditioning blasted across my face. "I hope you guys aren't kidnappers."

"We're not kidnapping you," a petite girl with blonde hair and innocent eyes said from the front seat, her brow furrowed with worry.

"She'll come to her senses," the driver said as we pulled back onto the road. "Just give her some water."

"My name's Anna," the blonde girl said. I opened one eye as she gave me an excited little wave. "What church do you go to?"

"Don't mind her," the driver said. "It's literally the first thing she asks every person she meets. I'm Layla. Freckles is Chloe."

"Amanda," I said.

The girl with the red hair nodded and said "Hey" as she pulled her seat belt back on.

"A person's faith says a lot about them," Anna went on. "It's a good conversation starter."

"I don't actually go to church any more." I felt a stab of guilt remembering how long it had been since I had gone to church, though I hoped God would understand why. "I used to go to Calvary Baptist, though, down near Atlanta."

Anna clapped and bounced in her seat. "She's a Baptist!" she said happily as the other girls rolled their eyes.

"How many people do you know in this town who aren't Baptists?" Layla said. "How many people in the whole South?"

"I know some Lutherans," Anna protested, squaring her shoulders.

"Here." Chloe handed me a water bottle from her backpack. I rasped a thank you and guzzled half the bottle, spilling water on my chin and shirt.

"You hungry?" Layla asked, turning to me from the front seat. "I bet she's hungry. Let's grab a bite."

A sign reading HUNGRY DAN's in garish neon letters hung above a 1950s-style restaurant covered with blinding chrome. I got my first good look at Layla and Anna as we left the car. Layla stood as tall as me, with black hair and creamy skin. Anna barely reached Chloe's shoulder, and her long, shimmering blonde hair flowed to the bottom of her red Bible Camp T-shirt.

Inside, framed posters for movies like *Grease* and *Rebel Without a Cause* hung on the two back walls, and menus with cracked fake leather binding and plastic covers lay on the table.

As the waitress took our orders I checked my phone and realized it was dead. I started to ask if I could borrow one of the other girls' phones to tell Dad I'd be home late, but then hesitated. I might still make it before he got back from work, and I didn't want to tell him I'd missed the bus on my very first day.

"So anyway," Layla said with an air of ceremony, "there's a football game this Thursday." She turned to me. "You're coming, right?"

"Ooh, yes," Anna agreed.

"I don't really like sports." I shrugged.

"But our best linebacker has a crush on you," Layla replied, smiling coyly.

"Who?"

"Parker," Chloe said. "You know him?"

"Oh, she knows him," Layla said, raising her eyebrows knowingly.

"I d-don't—" I stammered.

"There's no point playing dumb," Layla said, a fry held gingerly between her fingers like a cigarette. "Him and Grant sit by me in biology. I heard them talking about how you shot Grant down."

My cheeks burned as I remembered Grant's easy smile. "It wasn't like that." I shook my head. I wondered, for a moment, what my response would have been if Grant had asked me out for himself.

"Quit torturing her," Anna said. She turned to me.

"So how's Lambertville been for you so far? Everyone been nice?"

"It's okay," I said. "I mean, I've only met five people so far, including you guys and Grant."

Anna smiled. "Who's the fifth?"

"Her name's Bee. We have art together."

The girls exchanged a quick glance, their eyes meeting and then darting quickly away.

"What's wrong with Bee?" I asked.

"Nothin'," Chloe said.

"She's fun in small doses," Layla said. "Emphasis on the small."

I sucked at the dregs of my soda, unsure what to say.

"God, I'm a bitch," Layla said after a moment. "Hang out with whoever you want. We just met! But you're welcome with us anytime."

When the bill came, they refused to let me pay. I fell into the Southern ritual I'd watched Mom play out for years without even thinking: offer to pay once, they refuse, pull out your money and insist, they refuse again, and then concede. I wished all social interaction had such clear rules.

Twenty minutes later we pulled up outside my apartment building, an unimaginative tan brick box sitting beneath a tall ridge choked in kudzu vines.

"So you're coming to the game then, right?" Anna asked.

The cicadas buzzed persistently in the growing dusk. I had read once that they lived underground for most of their lives, only emerging as adults to live out their final days. Was that going to be me? Was I going to live underground for the better part of my life, never coming out into the world?

They were all looking at me hopefully, the car's engine running. Finally I said, "I'll meet you guys there."

Layla honked the horn happily, and they drove off.

After the car disappeared around the bend, I stood alone in the blistering parking lot. It was way past six, and Dad must have been home for a while, wondering where I was, with no way to reach me. I wanted to avoid whatever waited in the apartment, to wander around until midnight and sneak in once he fell asleep, but even at dusk the heat was still overpowering.

I climbed the stairs, turned the key in the lock, and stepped inside. Dark filled the space like a living thing. A single sunbeam came in through the gap in the balcony blinds and cut across the living room, red dust motes floating in a golden sea.

"Where were you?" Dad walked into the light, a hard edge in his voice.

"Sorry," I said quietly.

"Sorry isn't a place."

"With some friends," I said, looking down. "I missed the bus."

"When I got home and you weren't here I called over and over. I was worried sick."

I started to speak, choked, and took a deep breath. "You never worried before." I remembered the days after I woke up in the hospital and realized I was still alive. I remembered having nobody to keep me company but nurses and Mom and the television – no friends, no family, no Dad. I remembered suspecting, for the first time in my life, that he might not actually care if I lived or died.

I clenched my fists and looked up at him. "You never even sent a letter. I almost died and you were a ghost."

"What did you want me to say?"

"Anything."

He sighed, letting out his breath long and slow.

"I didn't know what to do, okay?" he said, rubbing his brow. "You hold a baby when it takes its first breath, you sing it to sleep, you rock it when it cries, and then you look away for what feels like a second and your baby doesn't want to live any more. You're my *child*."

"I'm your *daughter*," I whispered. "Nothing to say about that, either."

A semi drove by on the highway outside, the dull whoosh of its passing loud in the silence. "Sorry for worrying you. It won't happen again." I moved past him towards my room, closing the door.

NOVEMBER, THREE YEARS AGO

The counsellor's office was a converted study in an old mansion in one of the Atlanta neighbourhoods rebuilt soonest after the Civil War. It smelled like old wood, and the floors creaked with a century of traffic. An old television sat on a rolling stand in the mouth of a fireplace large enough to swallow it whole. Embellished shelves meant for leather-bound books were lined with titles like, *I'm OK, You're OK* and *Coping with PTSD*. A grandfather clock echoed persistently outside the door.

The counsellor tapped his pen against his notepad, maddeningly out of sync with the rhythm of the clock. I pulled my knees up to my chest and tried to disappear into the overstuffed leather chair.

"How are you, Andrew?"

"I don't know," I said. I pulled mechanically at a loose thread in my jeans.

"What would you like to talk about?"

"Nothing," I said.

"Could I ask you a question?"

"If you want."

He uncrossed his legs and rested his hands in his lap. He was using his body language to tell me I could trust him, because it was his job to seem trustworthy. When he spoke his tone was calm and even. "Will you tell me about the note you gave me when you were in the hospital?" I closed my eyes and shrugged. "Could you tell me what the note meant?"

"I like puzzles," I said after a moment. My knuckles blocked my mouth, muffling my words. He leaned closer to hear. "And science. I like things that fit together neatly. I don't like it when things don't make sense." I put my hands on the back of my neck and pushed my head down, speaking into my lap. "So I don't know what the note meant. It means I'm crazy, I guess, because it doesn't make sense."

"What doesn't make sense, Andrew?"

"My birth certificate says I'm a boy." My chest felt tight. The room, despite its high ceilings, felt suddenly cramped. "I have a…I have boy parts. I have boy chromosomes. God doesn't make mistakes. So I'm a boy. Scientifically, logically, spiritually, I'm a boy."

He steepled his fingers and leaned even further forward. "It sounds like you're trying to convince yourself. Something tells me you aren't like other boys."

"I know I like boys," I said. I stared up at the ceiling and jiggled my foot rapidly. "You don't have to be a girl to like boys, though."

"Is there anything specific to being a boy that bothers you?"

"Clothes," I said quickly. I had never said these things out loud. My ears were ringing. My skin felt too tight. "I've wanted to wear girl clothes for as long as I can remember."

"Have you ever done it?"

"When I was in first grade, the girl next door let me. Her parents caught us and I wasn't allowed to go back."

He made an ambiguous sound in his throat and I heard him jot something on his pad.

"So when you wrote 'I should have been a girl', did you mean that you're afraid to come out as gay, or embarrassed that you want to wear women's clothes? Your mother said you're Baptists; do you think the way you feel is wrong from a religious perspective?"

"No," I said. "I don't think God actually cares about that kind of thing, and I think I could deal with just being gay or whatever. It feels wrong that I'm a boy, though. When my hair gets long and people mistake me for a girl, I feel happy. I try to imagine what kind of man I'll grow up to be, and nothing comes. I think about being a husband or a father and even if it's with a man I feel like I'm being sucked into a black hole. The only time

I feel like I have a future at all is if I imagine I'm a girl in it."

"I see," he said. I heard more scratches as he wrote more notes. "Gender identity disorder is in the most current diagnostic manual," he said. "It's a real thing that lots of people experience."

I forced myself to make eye contact with him. He was no longer leaning forward. He was sitting back, feet together, hands in his lap again.

"I have it?"

"I'm not really prepared to diagnose anything at this point," he said. "And I have to wait until I've taken a look at your questionnaires, but if you don't have major depressive disorder and panic disorder I'll eat my hat."

"You don't wear a hat," I said. He winked, and I smiled despite myself. "What happens next?"

"I'm going to refer you to a psychiatrist to see about some medicine for your anxiety and depression. I also want you to do something this Saturday, if you aren't busy."

"I don't really have friends," I said.

"We'll see how long that lasts," he replied. "There's a small support group that meets here at six on the first Saturday of the month. I think you should come."

CHAPTER FOUR

By the time I reached the football field on Thursday after school, cars filled the dust-choked parking lot. Parents and teachers milled outside the field, their long shadows hinting at the coming autumn.

Anna greeted me with a warm smile, her blonde hair pulled back into short pigtails.

"Game doesn't start for a bit," she said as Layla strode into view, looking underdressed in a black T-shirt and black aviators.

"Hey!" she said. "What did I miss? You tell her Parker still has the hots for her yet?"

"No," Anna said, shifting her feet uncomfortably. "It ain't my place."

I felt red splotches run up my neck. Parker seemed harmless enough, but something about him made me uncomfortable. He reminded me too much of guys who had beaten me and thrown me in lockers for so much of my life.

"Where's Chloe?" Layla flipped her short bob.

"Not sure. I thought she'd meet us here, but I guess she'll just find us in the stands."

We passed through the gap in the fence near the bleachers. The athletic equipment shone with a surprising cleanness and the grass was lush and even. Too many dads seemed interested in us as we passed, and for just a moment I missed the near-invisibility of life as a boy.

I noticed Grant as we passed the bench. He gave me a wide, lopsided smile, the same smile he'd been giving me whenever our eyes met in homeroom or the halls. "Amanda! Hey!"

"I'll save you a seat," Layla said, pushing me towards him. I stepped forwards gingerly, reminding myself that there was nothing to be afraid of.

"You came."

"I did."

"Do you even like football?"

"No," I admitted, shaking my head and laughing. "Why, is there something else to do in this town?"

"Ouch!" He put his hand over his heart, but then turned more serious. "Don't know if you've heard, but some people are gettin' together Saturday night. Think you might wanna come?"

Saturday night. I thought about what Saturday night

had looked like for the last ten years. Dinner with my mom: Chinese takeout if we were feeling adventurous; pork chops with cornbread, black-eyed peas and turnip greens if we weren't. Video games in my room: all alone, late into the night, until my fingers ached and I was tired enough to fall asleep without my thoughts swirling. An actual high school party had always been a distant, exotic thing, something that only existed in movies.

I nodded slowly. "I could do that, I think."

"Well, all right then," he said, smiling and scratching his temple.

Parker sauntered over from the bench and handed Grant his helmet.

"Game's about to start," he said. He glanced at me quickly, and turned away.

"Sorry." Grant shrugged. "Gotta go."

He grinned as he trotted over to the bench.

Layla and Anna looked ready to explode when I joined them in the bleachers.

"I think Parker has competition," Anna said, smiling brightly and twisting her long, blonde hair in her fingers.

"Three words." Layla raised a finger in the air. "Awkward. Dorky. Adorable. I loved it."

I smiled so hard my cheeks hurt. I felt, at least for a moment, what it was like to be a normal teenage girl.

* * *

By the end of the first quarter I desperately needed to pee. I glanced behind the bleachers to where the bathrooms stood, two low, squatting buildings, one bearing the telltale stick figure in a skirt. I had only used a women's room a few times since I'd been attacked, and the idea still made my heart race. But there was no avoiding it now.

"Want company?" Layla asked as I excused myself.

"No," I said quickly. Layla leaned back and pursed her lips. "Sorry. I'm fine, thanks."

I left the bleachers and headed for the bathrooms. When I pushed open the door, the smell of paint and bleach invaded my nostrils, reminding me how much cleaner girls' bathrooms were than boys'. The stalls were empty, and I let out the breath I'd been holding. Outside two female voices whispered back and forth, their words too soft to make out. One giggled. I washed up quickly and as I exited the bathroom, I found Bee and Chloe rounding the far corner. They stopped mid-stride. I froze with my still-damp hands mid-wipe on my thighs. Bee nodded in my direction. Chloe's eyes widened. Her fingers curled and uncurled at her side. She kept her eyes locked on the field, never turning them to me.

"Hey!" I said, forcing a conversational tone as if we'd just met in the halls. I couldn't tell what they were hiding; drugs, probably, but I also didn't really want to know. "Anna and Layla are near the benches, you can't miss them."

"Thanks," Chloe said. She glanced at me as she walked away, her red curls bouncing and her face as stony and unreadable as always. "Glad you came."

When it was just me and Bee, I turned to her. "I didn't think you were the football type."

"I'm not," Bee said. "I come here to watch great apes in their natural habitat." She unwrapped some gum and slowly put it in her mouth. "Enjoy the game."

"Okay," I said, wondering if "great apes" applied to just the athletes or to everyone, and if that generalization of the popular kids included me. "See you later."

When I returned, Chloe was between Anna and Layla, leaning back on her elbows and looking down on the game below. Our gaze met as I climbed the bleachers and she went stiff again. I waved, pretending it was the first time we'd seen each other. She mouthed *thank you* as I sat down.

As the girls went back to talking, my attention drifted to the field below. I'd never sat through an entire game before; football was something I associated with the great apes, as Bee called them, the people who'd dedicated their lives to destroying mine. But today, the sound of the girls' happy chatter washing over me, sun glinting off the bleachers, and the smell of fresh-cut grass in the air, I couldn't help enjoying it. At the end of the third quarter, when Grant ran the ball into the end zone, I stood and cheered until my voice grew hoarse.

I wondered what Dad would think if he knew I was watching sports of my own free will. I remembered when I quit Little League after the first game and cried in my room, how angry and disappointed he had been. This felt different from Dad and all of his buddies – always buddies, never really friends – sitting around quietly watching "the game" with beers in hand. This felt like something else, like friendship or acceptance or maybe fitting in. This felt like fun.

CHAPTER
FIVE

On Friday I found Bee behind the art building like always. She slouched against the wall, eyes closed, bobbing her head in time to the music blasting in her ears. My backpack thudded into the grass and I joined her. She opened one eye and wiggled her fingers in greeting.

"What are you listening to?"

"The Knife. They're this awesome Swedish experimental...thing. Here, listen." She handed me the earbud and leaned in so I could share. I held it to my ear. I expected a cross between ABBA and Daft Punk, but instead a low, soulful voice sang about doomed love.

"So I heard Grant's all about you," Bee said once the song ended.

"It's nothing," I said, even though the thought made my heart pound. "He just invited me to a party."

"He's a guy," she said. "You're new and you're pretty.

It's not exactly rocket science."

"I'm not pretty though."

"Oh my God, whatever, yes you are. Jesus. The only thing worse than attractive people is attractive people who refuse to admit they're attractive."

"I don't think we're making good use of our time," I said, but I was fighting a smile. I doubted anyone but Bee could make a compliment sound so grouchy. "I mean, if we get caught I'd like to point to some projects we've done and say, 'We used art class to make art.'"

"Insanely naïve, but I'm bored so I'm still with you."

"Okay, so I spent last night on Pinterest getting ideas," I said, pulling out my phone.

"Of course you've got a Pinterest. I bet you've already planned like three different wedding themes." Bee grabbed the phone from my hand and swiped at the screen, her brow knitted. "Half these are pine-cone jewellery. This isn't art," she said, handing me back the phone. "This is crafts. They're different."

"It's called arts and crafts."

"Art," Bee said, slipping her feet back into her shoes, "expresses something deeply personal and private. Art shares your world with other people so they can feel even a momentary connection with you. Crafts are pine-cone hats."

"I didn't pin any pine-cone hats," I said indignantly, reaching into my backpack and pulling out an old sketchbook with a few blank pages left. Bee sat up and looked over my shoulder. "I sketched some designs you might like more—"

"Go back," she said. I went back one page, to a piece of Sailor Moon fan art I'd drawn two years before. I thought it looked amateurish and tried to turn the page away, but Bee put her hand over mine and stopped me. "You drew this?"

I nodded. "It's just fan art. Nothing original."

"Stop," Bee said. "There are enough people waiting to crap in your cereal without you doing it for them. You're talented." She stood up and scratched her back where her bare skin had touched the grass. "Come with me."

I took a deep breath and followed her to the parking lot. She unlocked a worn-looking red pickup truck and hopped in the driver's seat.

"Where are we going?"

"You want to make art," she said. "So let's get serious. Art is about exposing yourself. I'm going to share some things with you. You don't have to share anything with me unless you want to, you know, create something worth creating." She lit a cigarette as she started the car and blew a grey cloud into the wind.

"You can't tell anybody what I'm about to show you," she said as we pulled inside a cemetery gate. "I mean you can, obviously, but I'm trusting you not to."

We parked and I followed her up the hill along the main path. Eventually it opened onto an overgrown clearing.

I shielded my eyes and saw a run-down plantation house, its windows shattered and its paint long peeled away.

"This is my place," Bee said. "I come here to get some privacy and develop my photos."

"It's creepy," I said, rubbing my arms despite the pleasant weather.

"I know, right? I looked it up in the town hall – nobody's lived in it since the 50s."

The grass pushed back like water as we walked. "Why was it abandoned?"

Bee lit another cigarette, cupping her hand around the flame as a strong wind kicked up. Her cheeks sucked in as she shrugged. "Damned if I know."

The wind gathered strength, rippling across the grass. I looked up at the first-floor balcony, with its darkened windows and pillars disintegrating from rot. For the first time all summer the cicadas' song completely faded. The world felt bigger and lonelier than it had a moment before.

"I found some graves out in the woods last year," she said.

"You think they buried slaves there?"

"Or soldiers. They turned it into a hospital before the war ended. Can you feel it?" She sat on the porch's groaning top step as she finished her cigarette and removed a professional-looking camera from its case.

I stood a little way from the steps, still waist-high in the grass. Bee pointed her camera at me and clicked the shutter four times in quick succession. "I don't believe in ghosts," I told her.

"I didn't ask if you believe in ghosts," she said. She flicked her cigarette into a rusted-out bucket near the door and headed inside. An anxious shiver ran up my back as I followed her. "I asked you what you *feel*. You can't have art if you spend all your time forgetting pain."

Broken glass littered the floor inside. A small plastic table and a camping chair stood to the left, an electric lantern casting a bright ring in every direction. I wondered if Bee knew how privileged she was to be able to feel anything at all, if she knew just how scary numbness could be. How it felt, sometimes, like a darkened room with no way out.

"I want you to play the honesty game with me." The sky flashed outside and thunder rolled across the sky. I looked up and saw white and grey clouds hurrying past the sun as a shadowy line rushed across the clearing. Storms always followed a heatwave. The hotter it burned and the longer it lasted, the worse the storm would eventually rage. "Probably foreshadowing. The honesty game is intense." She walked into the other room and returned with a stool, gesturing for me to take the camping chair.

"What is it?" I said, already certain I didn't want to play. Outside, rain began to fall in a slate-grey sheet.

"It's Truth or Dare without the dirty shit, pretty much.

How it works is we take turns telling the other person something about us they probably don't know. You do it five times, starting with something dumb, then you escalate and, by the end, you share something you never thought you would tell anyone. The challenger – me – goes first. No matter what you say to me, you'll know I can't blab because you've got all my dirt."

"I don't think I want to." I fidgeted in the chair, biting my lip. I imagined all the things I couldn't tell her. Could never tell anyone.

"You don't have to," she said. She blew her hair back into place and reached for her pipe and a shimmering plastic baggy. She carefully stuffed dried green leaves into the bowl.

"Could I get high first?" I said, my hands balled in my lap.

She tilted her head. "I already think you're cool, you know. You don't need to smoke to impress me."

"No," I said. I imagined my insides taut like piano wire, humming as they prepared to snap. "I just want to…I want to relax. I haven't really relaxed since…well, since ever."

She nodded, once, and put the pipe and the lighter on the table between us.

"It doesn't always make you relax," she said. "For the record I don't think it's a good idea. I'm not your mom, though."

Two more thunderous peals growled at us before I worked up the courage to touch the wavy-lined blue-and-green pipe. Its glassy surface felt like the unicorn trinkets in Mom's bedroom. I almost laughed at the association as I picked it up and held it. The mouthpiece tasted warm and wet as Bee instructed me on how to do it.

"Don't cough yet," she said as smoke flooded my lungs. I held my lips shut. My chest heaved and my eyes watered. Finally the sizzle in my chest hurt too much and I let the coughs come. A blinding halo surrounded my head as I bent double, coughing long after my lungs were empty.

"I think I did something wrong," I said. "Nothing's happening."

"Everybody says that," Bee said. "Give it a sec."

I leaned back in the chair and closed my eyes, a tingling feeling beginning to spread through my body. I felt brave and free in a dizzy, nauseated way.

"So I guess it's up to me to start." Bee lit another cigarette and thought for a moment. "I competed in beauty pageants until five years ago."

A laugh sprung from my insides, buzzing through my lips before finally breaking free.

"If you weren't high I'd take offence."

"I'm not high," I said. My voice sounded slow and warped, like it came through a pink toy-store bullhorn, which made me laugh even harder.

51

"You're high," she said. She waited for me to calm down and then handed me her phone. I took it, just barely getting my breathing under control. On the screen was a photo of a girl with long, bleached hair curled in perfect ringlets, wearing a silver sequined gown.

"I think you're a lot prettier now," I said. I meant it. A warm wave ran from my toes up to my head.

"Our peers disagree," she said. "Whatever. I could be her again if I wanted to be. They're jackasses for ever. Your turn."

"My ears aren't pierced." I remembered asking my parents when I was little, and how embarrassed and confused I'd felt when Dad responded angrily. My emotional life had already begun to collapse at that point, but something about that particular dressing-down knocked loose the floodgates, and months of bottled-up loneliness, fear and shame poured out. I remembered lying on my bed after Dad was done yelling at me, listening to the cardinals outside, and wondering if that was the last time I would ever cry, if God had decided I only got a set amount of tears in my whole life.

"Seriously? That's all you've got?"

"You said to start small!" I protested. "Okay fine. How's this instead? I've never been drunk."

"Well, you're high as shit right now, so I'd say you're well on your way. My turn: I've got to at least third base in every bathroom at school."

"With who?" I said, loud enough to startle myself. I started giggling again, but did a better job keeping it in check. "With whom, I mean. Whom." I liked the way "whom" felt in my mouth.

"Your turn," Bee said, shaking her head.

"Ohh-kay," I conceded, dragging the word out like a disappointed child. A bubble hovered at my mind's edge, waiting to pop. I existed in the moment, free from the past and the future. "I switched schools because someone beat me up. You can still feel the stitches above my ear."

She took a long drag on her cigarette, lighting the tip bright red, and held it for a while. "A year ago I spent a month at Valley down in Chattanooga."

"What's that?" I asked.

"Loony bin," she said, tapping her cigarette on the table's edge. Ash floated to the ground.

"I tried to kill myself my sophomore year," I said.

Her eyes widened. "How?"

"It was a few weeks after my mom broke her leg. Her prescription painkillers were sitting out. I took too many."

"How many's too many?"

"Whole bottle," I said, chewing my fingernails.

"Why, though?"

I just shook my head.

"I'm glad you didn't," Bee said. "Kill yourself, I mean." She met my eyes as she put her cigarette out on the table. "I'm bisexual."

"Really?" I said slowly, trying to fit this fact in with everything I knew about Bee. I wondered if any part of me had suspected. "Have you ever dated a girl?"

"Remember when you saw me and Chloe at the game?"

"Wow," I said, my eyebrows shooting up. I wondered if anyone else knew about Chloe. I doubted it; she was a little masculine, of course, but that didn't necessarily mean anything, and it didn't seem like anyone was out and proud at Lambertville High. "I thought maybe you were smoking."

"Nah," she said. "Chloe's a huge jock, so she refuses to corrupt her body or whatever."

I nodded, processing what she had told me. I had been so caught up with my own secret, I realized, it hadn't occurred to me that my new friends were keeping secrets of their own. We sat silently for a few moments, listening to the rain pound the roof. It reminded me of the time Dad took me hunting with some buddies from work and a freak storm kept us trapped in our cabin all weekend. I tried to make oatmeal cookies like in Mom's recipe book from the ingredients on hand, but all it seemed to do was make Dad uncomfortable. He never took me hunting again.

Bee's voice cut through the quiet. "Your turn. It's your fourth, so better make it a good one."

"Okay," I said, trying to control my breathing. "Just give me a minute, okay?" She shrugged.

I thought again of that weekend, and how I threw the cookies away even though there was nothing wrong with them. I thought of how I'd stopped doing so many of the things I'd enjoyed so Dad wouldn't be mad. I thought of going the rest of my life pretending I sprang to life from nothing at sixteen years old, and felt my cheeks flush with shame and anger. I was so tired of cowering. I was so tired of hiding. I *wanted* to tell the truth, to say it out loud.

But when I went to speak, nothing came out.

"I'm sorry," I said finally. My eyes felt dry. "I know what I need to say, but I just...can't."

She waited a moment. Lightning flashed outside the house. I expected her to prod me, or maybe try to guess. But she just leaned back and said, "The rain doesn't look like it's gonna let up anytime soon. Get your sketchbook."

I set the pad on my lap. "What should I draw?"

"Whatever you want."

I put a pencil to paper and licked my lips. Within a few seconds the outline of a sad-eyed little boy appeared. Minutes passed as I sketched, the only sound the pattering of the rain on the roof.

"It's okay, you know," Bee said quietly, taking a long drag of her cigarette. "Whatever it is you can't tell me." She met my eyes. "It's gonna be okay."

DECEMBER, THREE YEARS AGO

I was an hour early for the support group. The door was locked and the lights were off, so I crouched on the stoop. I played Final Fantasy on my handheld while I waited. My fingers were numb but my character in the game was named Amanda and she was beautiful and powerful, and watching her kill monsters helped calm me down. The only time I got to feel like myself was when I played pretend.

It was the first week of December, and every house but this one was draped in twinkling white lights like snow and ice. I had only seen snow twice before we moved, and it never snowed in Georgia. It was very cold, though, which was nice. When it was cold outside I could wear thick boots, thick jeans, sweaters, scarves and hats. I could cocoon myself so that the only visible parts of me were my nose and my eyes and a few strands of brown hair.

Nobody could tell if I was a boy or a girl.

"Well, hello," a voice called from the yard. I paused my game and looked up. A girl a few years older than me in black leather boots strode down the garden path towards the porch, waving. She was tall and long-legged, with a cloud of natural hair bouncing with every step. I put my handheld away and stood, tucking my hands under my armpits. "Are you new? I can't really tell."

"I am," I said. Even my voice was sexless when filtered through my wool scarf. "New, I mean. I haven't been here before."

"Good!" she said, beaming. She unlocked the front door and motioned me in. The front room was uncomfortably warm, but I didn't want to leave my cocoon yet. "I'm Virginia, by the way. Coffee?"

"You don't have to make me anything," I said. "I'll just get water."

She brought me to a kitchen that looked like something out of the 1940s, all white and blue tiles and high windows. I sat and sweltered while she ground coffee beans.

"Listen," she said, "by all means wear whatever makes you comfortable, but it's hot as Santa's butt crack in here and I just know you're cooking in there. I promise, whatever you're hiding, in this place, what we see is what you know you are inside."

I stood blankly for a second and then I took off my hat. My hair was damp and stringy with sweat. I unwrapped my scarf, the scratchy wool pulling at my skin like a Band-Aid.

Virginia smiled. "See? You're gorgeous."

She sat beside me and took my hands in hers. The size of her hands was the only thing that might have given her away, but next to my bony, pale fingers hers were beautiful and dark and alive. "Listen, a lot of the people you're going to see tonight are pretty…rough. Don't let them scare you off, okay?"

"Okay," I whispered.

"But don't treat them like freaks either," she said. "Just open your eyes and see them the way they really are. They're all beautiful, okay?" I nodded. She squeezed my hand.

I heard the door open and close, and voices drifted in from the front room. A short, round man with smooth, beardless cheeks and spiky blond hair swaggered in. Virginia introduced him as Boone and he waved with a grunt. He was followed by a girl with long, straight, shiny black hair and a ratty, patched overcoat that went past her knees. Virginia introduced her as Moira, but if she heard, she didn't say anything. The girl looked at her feet while she walked, and I wanted to tell her I understood, but part of understanding was knowing that telling her that would only make her nervous.

"Where's Wanda?" Virginia asked. She sat forwards in her chair, elbows tucked in and hands cradling her mug.

"Couldn't get a sitter," the man said. His voice was high and raspy. "Who's the kid?"

"What is your name, actually?" Virginia said, arching an eyebrow.

"Andrew," I said. My ribcage started to collapse. My heart thumped in my ears.

"Is that your real name?"

A woman with broad shoulders and a faint shadow of a beard under her make-up entered next. She looked strong and stout, but the longer I looked the more I saw the beauty in her – here a light step, here a brief touch of the hair, here a wide, open smile. Boone said, "Evening, Rhonda," to greet her.

"Amanda," I said then. "It's…I mean it's not my name, but I always wanted it to be. So, Amanda, I guess."

"Would you like it if we called you that?" Moira asked. Her dark-ringed eyes bore down on me, but the corners of her mouth turned up in a faint smile.

"I'm not sure," I said. My chest felt tight but warm and my breathing was shallow. "I think I want that."

"Well, then, I would like to introduce my friend Amanda to everyone," Virginia said, squeezing my hand and smiling. My eyes burned suddenly, and when I rubbed my cheek, my hand came away wet. I tried to remember the last time I had been able to cry.

CHAPTER
SIX

Anna insisted on giving me a ride to the party Saturday night. Dad and I had been avoiding each other for most of the week, but he actually looked like he might smile when she picked me up in front of the apartment complex in her family's green minivan. Maybe the religious bumper stickers stuck all over the van's backside like wallpaper reassured him I was making friends with the right people.

We pulled up to the house as the setting sun limned the western mountains in red and purple. The house was white and ranch-style, and looked like it could be on the cover of *Southern Living*. A garden overflowed with flowers in full bloom. I knew all of their names: Indian pinks, white rain lilies, Stokes' aster, false indigo. Mom had taught me them years before, until Dad found me gardening, and they fought.

Inside, music rattled the floors and kids were packed together tightly, big red paper cups in hand. A keg stood by the entrance to the kitchen, a line snaking around the corner. Chloe and Layla waved us over as soon as we walked in, giving us both hugs. In the last week I'd been given more hugs than in my entire life combined. I was anxious about anyone touching me and my reflex was to tense up and jump away, but once I took a deep breath and relaxed I found that I actually enjoyed it, that momentary contact that said you weren't alone.

Chloe directed me towards the kitchen, telling the other girls we'd get them drinks – beer for Layla and water for Anna, who didn't drink. I started to say I didn't drink either, but then I remembered I had got high the day before, and suddenly a beer hardly felt adventurous at all.

When it was just the two of us, Chloe leaned in close. "Thanks again," she said. "For Thursday."

"I have no idea what you're talking about," I told her with a smile.

She tapped her red cup against mine. "You know everybody here talks about how much other people talk," she said. I was pretty sure that was more words together than I had heard her use all week. "But the more they talk about how shameful it is, the more they do it."

Behind us, Layla and Anna were fiddling with our host's iPhone and speakers. They shrieked happily as a new song came on.

"If you ever want someone to talk to," I told her, "I know how to keep a secret."

Twenty minutes later I sat on a countertop staring out at the sea of people filling the house. Anna, Layla and Chloe were all talking to other people, so I tried to look busy as I sipped gingerly from my red plastic cup and tapped my heel in time with the Top 40 hits blaring over the speaker. I was unimpressed with beer – it tasted like stale bread and water, and it wasn't making me feel any different.

"Um…hey," a deep voice called, almost drowned out by the music and the crowd. I looked up and saw Parker, a nervous expression on his face.

"Hey," I said, trying to act nonchalant. Something about his heavy-lidded gaze always set me on edge. "Congrats on the game the other night."

"We lost."

"It was still the most fun I've ever had watching sports," I said, shrugging. "Seems like there should be a prize for that."

"Oh," he said, looking away. His cheeks flushed red and it occurred to me that he was *nervous*. I felt guilty all of a sudden, as if just by existing and talking to him I was leading him on. It gave me a strange sense of power, and not one that I liked.

"Can I get you a beer?"

"I already—" I began, but he said, "I'll go get you one" abruptly and disappeared into the crowd. I let out a long sigh as I watched him go.

Only seconds had passed when Grant appeared in front of me. He wore a heather-grey T-shirt and well-worn jeans, looking completely at ease, his jet-black hair tousled like he'd stuck his head out a car window on the freeway.

"So, hey," he said, giving me a mischievous smile. "I might be confused, but the idea of a party, generally, is to have fun."

"I'm having fun," I said, taking another sip of beer.

I had rehearsed this encounter all afternoon as I got ready. In the shower, I pretended I barely knew he existed, looking cool and aloof. As I blew out my hair, I threw caution to the wind and flirted mercilessly with him. While I got dressed, I gave innocent and naïve a shot. No more plans came to me when I got around to putting on make-up, and now that he was actually in front of me, I realized I didn't even have to try.

"You've been staring at the ceiling for the last ten minutes."

"Then you've clearly been staring at me."

"Can you blame me?" he said, shaking his head and laughing. "I just really wanna make sure you have a good time."

"I'm having a good time, I promise." I was starting to feel a little dizzy and realized the beer was finally having an effect. "I like this song a lot! It's, um, my favourite."

He raised an eyebrow. "Somehow I doubt anything by Kesha is your favourite."

"It could be!" He stared me down, plastering a maddeningly neutral look on his features. I broke in seconds. "Okay, fine. I only really listen to electronica."

"Come with me, then," he said, gesturing as he headed across the room. My head was buzzing pleasantly as I hopped down and followed him.

Out of the corner of my eye I caught Parker emerging from the kitchen, a red cup in each hand, craning his neck to look for me. The crowd parted at the other end of the room to reveal Grant swiping through the iPhone, his eyes intent on the screen. I tried to peek over his shoulder but he tapped the screen one last time, turned, and smiled at me triumphantly. The familiar, tinny beat of Daft Punk hit my ears, barely audible at first, but quickly building. Grant bit his lip and bobbed his head in time with the music. I finished my drink, set the cup on the table, and joined him.

The vocals kicked in, a digitized voice commanding me to work harder, become better, faster and stronger, reminding me my work was never over, and I felt so good, all of my fear gone somewhere else for the night. Grant took my hands, and I didn't shrink from his touch. Our fingers were the same length, I noticed, but his were much wider and stronger. He led me into the crowd, and when we took steps our feet moved in time with the beat, my hips following suit. Bodies pressed and swirled around me, but I didn't mind. Instinctively, I always avoided crowds, but tonight, the crush of bodies actually felt comforting. Dancing with a boy for the first time in my entire life, I felt like a part of the people around me, like another cell in a healthy body instead of a hidden disease.

The song ended abruptly and I realized I was dizzy and a little nauseated. I squeezed Grant's arm, smiled, and jerked my head towards the corner, trying to indicate that I needed a moment to breathe. He nodded, ran his strong fingers through his wild hair, and grinned.

Crushed by the crowd, I navigated to a back wall, leaning against it. As I took long, even breaths, trying to slow my racing heart, my eyes were drawn to a photo on the mantel, of a dozen young boys rough-housing on a log. One of them must have been our host, but the one on the far right was clearly Grant, and his arms were wrapped around a smaller, light-haired boy I found myself staring at. They both had sunburned cheeks and dripping-wet hair, their faces wide with huge, earnest smiles. I wondered who the other boy was. Did Grant have a brother I didn't know about yet?

"Here she is!" Layla cried as she appeared before me, whirling through the crowd with ease. Chloe followed, hands in pockets and elbows out, the crowd parting for her.

"Thought we'd lost you," Anna said, her hair messy from being jostled.

"I figured one of her admirers whisked her away," Layla replied, raising her eyebrows suggestively.

I noticed Parker and Grant across the room, deep in conversation, and wondered what they were talking about. I realized I didn't want to think about it, so I held up the photo instead. "Who is this?"

"Some kid Grant knew back in the day," Layla replied. "They were pretty inseparable, I remember."

"I recognize him – they went to my church," Anna said. Her eyes looked pained. "Him and his dad came every Sunday. The mom stayed home. He always seemed really sad, but my parents wouldn't let me talk to him. Bad influence."

Layla lowered her voice. "I heard the kid was really sick. Like, terminal. That's why they moved away."

Parker broke in, grabbing the photo from my hand. "You talking about Tommy? Grant's little gay boyfriend?" Two of his enormous buddies appeared behind him. Suddenly the space felt stifling. "I heard his mom went full psycho, killed the dad and little Tom-Tom with a shotgun, then turned it on herself, and their heads were so messed up the coroner had to use their teeth to identify 'em."

Chloe narrowed her eyes and pursed her lips. Anna looked down at her feet.

"Park," Grant said, joining the circle. Parker turned

66

around. Grant's hands were in his pockets, his jaw set in a hard line. "Don't say shit like that, okay?"

Parker scowled and stood up straight, squaring his shoulders so he took up as much space as possible. His gaze drifted from Layla to Chloe, who were both staring straight ahead. Finally, he turned to look at me, a snide smile in his eyes.

"Yo, Grant," he said. "The new girl know you've got a vagina?"

I flinched as if I'd been struck. I wondered why people still made comments like that. I wondered when I'd stop caring. I took a step back and away.

But neither of them was looking at me. Grant just shook his head. "Have another drink, bud."

"Five bucks says she won't compare to your ex-boyfriend," Parker spat. He brushed his shoulder and headed for the keg, body-checking Grant on the way. His minions followed. Grant stayed put, not saying a word.

Someone turned the music back up, and soon the normal party sounds returned. Around me, people went back to talking and laughing and flirting and dancing. But I couldn't be one of them any more. I'd been crazy to think I ever could. When no one was looking, I slipped through the crowd and out the back door.

ELEVEN YEARS AGO

I wrote a good story at school. Mrs Upton told me my parents needed to see this story and to take it home right now, tonight. The story was for an assignment where we were supposed to imagine what we would be like when we were grown up, which was something I had thought about a lot.

In the story I found a car in my room like the one from *The Phantom Tollbooth* except purple instead of red because purple was my favourite colour and also it was a time machine instead of a machine to go to magical worlds. I got in the car and turned the key and drove and I arrived in the future! And in the future I was in a science lab and there was a very tall and pretty lady there with long hair who was busy working on her computer. She was wearing a lab coat but it was also a very pretty dress in a way that was hard to explain, so I drew a picture. The lady got up and hugged me and said that she was me, grown-up! She showed me how she drank a special medicine so that when she grew up she became a woman instead of a man. She told me that the way I felt like a girl inside of me was a true thing, and was not bad or wrong. Then I got in my time machine and came home.

I read the story again while I waited. The line for car pickups was very long, and normally I did not care because I was very patient, a real cool customer Dad said, but I wanted to show my story to my parents and that made waiting hard. I just knew Dad would be so happy when he found out he had a daughter and not a son, but maybe he would also feel silly that he and Mom made such a silly mistake? When he tried to do boy things with me he always frowned and stopped, so I did not think he wanted a son really, which was fine because I hated sports.

The pickup lady in the orange vest called my name and pointed to our brown station wagon three lanes back. I started to run, but the lady in the orange vest told me to slow down, which was a rule for my safety. I walked slowly between the other cars, but really I was wondering what kinds of clothes Mom and Dad would get me now. Hopefully some skirts since the weather was hot and jeans were so bad, the worst! I climbed into my booster seat and buckled myself in, which I learned to do without even being asked. Dad was driving the car, and Mom was not in the car, which was normal. They did not like riding in the car together because it made them full of stress and then they yelled, which I did not like.

"How was school?" Dad asked.

"Good!" I said. Dad nodded and turned on some music. I wanted to tell him about my story right away, but it was not safe to drive and read and if I read it to him he would not see the pictures. I hummed along to the song and bobbed my head but I did not kick my feet because that noise distracted Dad, which was *not* a safe thing to do. Finally we pulled into the driveway.

"Dad!" I said. "Dad, look what I did today! I wrote a whole story!" I ran around to his side of the car.

"Did you now?" he said. He smiled a little bit and since I did not see him smile often, I thought that was a good sign. Dad liked books, so I thought he would like my story. "I bet you'll be the next Faulkner."

He took the story from my hands and smiled when he read the cover. He smiled at the first page where I found the car. He smiled at the second page where I drove the car. He looked confused on the third page where I saw the beautiful lady. Then he frowned. My tummy felt sick and suddenly I wanted my story back. I was too scared to move though because he reached the page where the lady explained that she was me, and the lines were on his forehead like when he was very angry. He skipped the last three pages and read the note the teacher attached instead.

"Why does your teacher think you were being serious?"

he asked. He looked at me and I felt like I had not had a bath for days, but in my insides instead of my outsides. "This is a joke, right?"

I wanted to lie to Dad and I wanted to tell him the truth, and I did not know that a person could want two things like that at the same time. I looked at my shoes and felt myself starting to cry, which was a bad thing because Dad said crying was for girls, but I knew I was a girl but Dad thought that was a joke and he seemed angry about it and thinking about that made me cry even harder. Dad kneeled and put his hands on my shoulders.

"Look at me," he said. I shook my head. "Look at me!" he repeated, and his hands squeezed my shoulders. I wanted to close my eyes but I had already made him so angry. I did not want to be bad or in trouble. "You need to tell me this was a joke."

"Yes, sir." It was what I said when an adult was angry with me and I wanted them to stop being angry. He let go of my shoulders and put his hands on his knees. I sniffled and wiped my eyes and looked back up at him, but he was looking at the sky. He took a deep breath.

"Son," he said, "I want you to have a good life. Boys who really think the things in your story are confused. They don't have good lives. So you're not one of those boys."

"Yes, sir," I whispered.

He messed up my hair and smiled again, but the smile

did not reach his eyes. "I don't want to hear anything else about this, okay?"

"Yes, sir," I said.

"Come on, cheer up," he said. I sniffled and looked at the ground. "Let's go play catch, okay? Take your mind off it."

"No, thank you," I said, adding, "sir" before I went inside.

CHAPTER
SEVEN

As I walked away from the party, I took deep, calming breaths of crisp night air. The sun had set, and the stars were out. I still wasn't used to how crisp and clear they looked here. Smyrna wasn't in the city proper, but Atlanta's light pollution reached a long way, leaving the sky a blue-and-purple smear. Out here you could make out everything, even the dim band of the Milky Way. I wished I could walk up into the sky and live on some distant planet, far away from the things I was afraid of. I wondered if joy could ever be felt by itself without being tainted with fear and confusion, or if some level of misery was a universal constant, like the speed of light.

"Hey." I was halfway down the block when I heard a voice behind me. I turned to see Grant, standing in the middle of the empty street. "Leaving already?"

"I'm not feeling great..." I trailed off. I desperately

wanted to finish the sentence with the truth, but what was there to say? *I think I like you, but I'll never have a normal life. I think you like me, but you'll never understand who I am.*

Grant pulled out a flashlight and flicked it on. We both blinked at the sudden radiance.

"Come with me?"

He turned towards the woods, and my feet knew before my brain did that I was going to follow. I was never going to be free of my past; it was always going to be there, waiting to suck me in and crush me like a black hole. The only way to escape it was to keep moving.

As we walked deeper into the woods, the short grass quickly gave way to grasping, thigh-high yellow blades. "That thing with Parker..." I began, thinking about how Grant had stood his ground. I wondered how many more times he would have to come to my rescue before I disappeared like Tommy. How many more friends would he have to alienate? "Will you guys still talk after this?"

Grant shrugged as the flashlight's beam illuminated a path for me to follow. "It would all blow over if we just had it out real quick after school," he replied evenly. "But he's huge, and mean, and so this stupid thing's probably gonna go on for months."

He paused as we approached a waist-high thicket of poison ivy. "Think you can jump it?"

"Not really," I said, still a little dizzy from the beer.

"Mind if I lift you?"

"I think so," I said, my throat going dry. I touched my fingers to my neck. "I think it's okay, I mean."

He laughed and grabbed my hips, easily carrying me over the ivy. I felt warm where his hands had touched me.

We kept walking, Grant still leading the way. The path opened onto a lake glimmering with faint white slivers. A chorus of frogs joined the cicadas' call, singing in their own asynchronous rhythm.

"I think boys aren't taught that smart's the same as scared sometimes," I said.

"You may be right." He pointed the flashlight up. "We're here." A tilted wooden platform nestled atop three thick tree branches. Clumsy, mismatched boards nailed into the trunk below served as a ladder.

"Where is here?" I asked. He looked sheepish.

"You'll see." He climbed up onto the platform and shone the flashlight down. I blinked. "Do you trust me?" He reached down and offered me his hand.

"Did you just quote *Aladdin*?" I took his hand and he easily hoisted me up.

I crawled over to the edge of the platform. From above, the lake reflected the moon clearly, a perfect white circle against its shimmering surface. I took a deep breath and turned to find Grant sitting with his back against the tree trunk.

"Thanks for coming out here with me," he said.

"Thanks for bringing me." I breathed in the cool lake air and sighed. "Do you live near here or something?"

"No," Grant said, looking suddenly cagey. "I, uh, used to. This was Tommy's old hideaway."

"Your friend?"

"Yeah. We used to come out here, when his folks fought or somebody screwed with him at school."

"What really happened to him?"

Grant rubbed his thumb over his fingertips. "He died."

I nodded silently. "Did he do it himself, or did somebody do it to him?"

"If people drive you to something," Grant whispered, his voice quaking slightly, "then it's their responsibility."

I couldn't breathe. I wanted to let him know how much it meant to have found someone out here, in this place, who would stand up for someone like Tommy, who would stand up for someone like the boy I used to be. I leaned forwards, searching with my fingertips, and slid my hand into his.

"You were a good friend," I said.

He squeezed my hand and for a long moment we listened to the wind on the lake and the frantic buzz of cicadas as life prepared for its long, cold sleep.

"Thanks," he said after a while. He put the flashlight down and lay on his belly, his upper body disappearing over the edge. "You know how to swim, right?"

"Yes," I said. Swimming had been the only exercise I

liked after puberty turned my body against me. Floating and darting through the water, I escaped the horrible tethers of my physical body. "I don't have a suit, though."

"Don't worry," he said, scampering down and out of sight. There was a momentary rustling and then his white undershirt soared over the tree house and landed at my feet. I stripped to my underwear quickly and pulled his shirt over my head – Grant wasn't that much taller than me, but boy clothes were so loose and baggy that the shirt came down low enough to cover everything.

"Don't lose that dress," I said as Grant climbed back up. "It's my favourite."

"It looks good on you," he replied. I fell silent as he hoisted himself back onto the platform and stood to his full, lean, shirtless height. He caught me staring and blushed. The tension broke as he exploded into motion, leaping off the edge. He hung suspended for a moment, arms spinning wildly, before straightening out and piercing the water's surface with a whisper.

I held my breath for a few tense seconds before he surfaced, laughing.

"You could've broken your neck!" I cried, putting my hands on my hips. "Do you know how many people get spinal injuries from bad dives every year?"

He wiped his eyes and slicked his hair back, treading water gracefully. "No," he said, catching his breath. "How many?"

"Well," I said as I stood, "I don't know either. But I bet it's a lot."

He laughed as I walked back towards the tree.

"I'm going to jump," I announced.

"I don't think—" he began, but I started running before he could finish. I reached the edge and took off. For one joyous moment, I felt weightless and free. And then came the burning slap as I hit the lake flat on my back.

"Ow," I croaked, floating to the surface.

"I tried to warn you," Grant said, swimming over.

"It's fine," I said, closing my eyes and feeling the pain radiate through my body. I didn't mind it; pain reminded me I was alive. For years I had been so numb, desperate to feel anything at all.

I opened my eyes and stared up, watching the stars turn overhead. A firefly buzzed urgently above my forehead, pulsing brightly to attract a mate. I sighed and gently paddled my feet, all my fear from earlier melting away.

Finally, after what could have been minutes or hours, Grant paddled towards the shore. He strode smoothly out of the water, not showing any sign of fatigue, and stared at me as I emerged.

"What?" I asked, looking down and panicking when I saw the thin white T-shirt sticking to my black bra. I crossed my arms over my chest and felt my face colour.

"You're beautiful."

I blinked in surprise. No boy had ever told me that before.

He grabbed my hand and we began the walk to my apartment. Reeds gave way to cut grass, and soon we were on a sidewalk. Street lamps glowed through the trees.

"You know what I'm gonna ask you, right?" Grant said. "Because I'd like to kiss you right now."

My heart caught in my chest. "Really?"

"We don't have to," he said quickly. "I know what you said before, about not being able to date…"

"No," I said. I leaned over and placed my hand on his. "I mean stop worrying. Yes. I mean yes."

He started to say something else but I closed my eyes and leaned towards him. He touched my face and met me halfway. Our lips were beaded with lake water. The kiss only lasted for a moment, but my mouth was numb and warm all at once.

He took my hand again and we finished the walk to my apartment in a pleasant, comfortable silence, my whole body singing with joy.

Except, a voice in my head whispered, *he would never have done this if he knew the truth.*

"Is something wrong?" he said, giving me a concerned look. I realized I'd been lost in thought.

"Oh," I said. "No. Nothing's wrong."

"It was a bad kiss, wasn't it?" He groaned.

"No, it was great. It's something else." I hadn't expected

this, hadn't planned for it, wasn't ready yet. But my lips were still warm from the kiss, and I felt more alive than I ever had. Happier than any medication had ever made me. Maybe I would never be ready; maybe I had to leap off the dock even if it meant falling flat moments later. Maybe I had to just let go. "I just…I like you." It felt like a relief to finally say something true.

"I like you too," he said. We stopped by my stairwell and laughed like happy idiots, our fingers laced together.

"I have to go, okay?" He sneaked another quick kiss and then we pressed our foreheads together, our faces only inches apart. Finally, he let me go.

"I'd like to call you tomorrow," he said.

"I'd like that," I said. "My phone's still at the tree house. Bring it here and we'll trade numbers."

"Okay." Grant smiled and backed away without turning, as though I might disappear if he looked away.

I walked upstairs and turned on the landing to wave at him. He remained in place, silently watching. I waved again, not wanting the moment to end, before he smiled and started the long walk to his car.

I ran a hand through my hair and whispered, "Shit."

I found Dad asleep on the couch, a DVR menu bathing him in blue light.

"Daddy?" I said softly, unafraid to use the word this

80

once because I knew he wouldn't hear me. "I'm home." He grunted and his eyes fluttered. He looked at me for a long moment with half-lidded, bleary eyes, and sounded far off when he spoke.

"Andrew?"

My heart nearly shattered. But then I remembered I was wearing Grant's shirt, that the light was low and he was half-asleep. I thought of *Sandman* and wondered if the son he wanted waited for him in Dream's kingdom every time he slept. I couldn't blame him.

"It's Amanda," I said softly.

"Amanda?" He blinked slowly and leaned in close. "Why are you wet? Whose clothes are those?"

"I went swimming with friends," I said. "Didn't have a suit, so I wore this."

"Oh," he said, stretching and yawning again. His back popped. "Good. It's bad to be alone."

"Let's get you in bed." I put his arm over my shoulder and immediately recognized the smell of whiskey.

"You're a good kid," he said, a faint slur in his voice. "Daughter. Sorry. I'm so sorry."

"It's fine."

"You look happy," he said.

"I think I am."

"I want you to smile. I love you."

Did he realize it had been a decade since he'd said those words? "I love you too," I replied. He pulled me into

81

a tight hug and kissed my cheek before I could react, then stumbled off to bed.

I closed his door and stood in the hall for a long time. The television buzzed, the vent fans whirred, and cold water soaked into the carpet around my feet as I replayed those three words in my head. I touched my fingers to my cheek, still the littlest bit raw from his stubble.

I remembered how angry he had sounded when he told me that lives like mine weren't good, couldn't possibly be good. I felt the scar above my ear and thought about how warm and tingly my lips still felt from Grant's kisses. I prayed that Dad had been wrong.

CHAPTER EIGHT

My phone chirped as I made my way through a sea of students rushing the front doors in preparation for the weekend. I sidled into one of the few empty spots by the office and pulled it out, hoping it was one of the girls saying their Friday-night plans had fallen through and they could hang out. Instead I saw Grant's name and the first few sentences of another of his texts.

"Hey!" the message read. "Sorry to keep bugging you, it's just I really liked what happened the other night and I thought you did too. I hope you'll—" I took a deep breath, closed my eyes, and put my phone away without reading the rest. The night of the party had been a mistake, a complete violation of the rules I'd set for myself – my plan, the whole reason I'd come to Lambertville. It was stupid, it was risky, and it couldn't happen again. Grant had been texting me ever since, and I'd been steadfastly ignoring him and avoiding him in the halls. I debated blocking his number to spare myself the temptation of responding, but for some reason I couldn't.

At least the weather was nice. I descended the steps and turned away from the buses, making my way around the school to the football field. It seemed a shame to waste a day like this even if I had to spend it alone, and Dad had agreed when I texted him at lunch to pick me up once he got off work. I climbed the bleachers and opened my *Catalogue of American Fiction* textbook to "A Good Man Is Hard to Find" by Flannery O'Connor. I immediately hated the old woman in the story, though it was pretty obvious I was supposed to. Part of me could sympathize with the bizarre standards she held herself to, to make sure people knew she was "a lady", but it was a small part. I was highlighting a line when my phone suddenly erupted in the *Star Wars* theme. I pulled it out and saw Grant was calling. The ringtone finished once and looped back to the beginning before I gave in and accepted the call.

"Hey," I said, trying to sound distant.

"So. Your phone ain't broke," Grant replied.

"No," I said, rubbing the bridge of my nose in anticipation of the next logical question: *why hadn't I responded to his texts?*

"And you like *Star Wars*?" he went on. "That's badass. I love *Star Wars*. Which one's your favourite?"

"*Empire Strikes Back*," I said reflexively, before sitting up straight and looking around. "Wait, how'd you know that?"

"Aw shit, *Empire*'s my favourite too! Look behind you." I turned and saw him sitting on the highest bench, a duffel bag over one shoulder and a phone to his ear. He grinned, flashing perfectly white teeth, and waved like a little kid.

"What?" I said, as I stuffed my things back in my bag and stood. "How did you…"

"I just came up on the far end over there," he said, pointing off to the side. "You were so into whatever you're reading I could've run up and down the field naked and you wouldn't've known."

"Are you stalking me?"

"Naw," Grant said, shrugging. "I accidentally left some stuff down by the benches after practice yesterday and saw you when I came to get it."

"Oh."

"I'm glad I ran into you though," he said. "You've been runnin' outta homeroom before I can even say hey, and I ain't seen you in the cafeteria all week."

"I was eating lunch out here," I said, rubbing my arm and looking away. "The weather's been nice."

"And my texts?" he said, as he descended the bleachers in long, loping strides. "I thought you liked me. You can tell me if you don't. I can handle rejection."

"No," I said, scooting over on the bleachers. "I mean yes.

85

I do. It's just…do you remember the conversation we had when you asked me out for Parker?"

"Ah," Grant said, sitting down next to me with his duffel bag between his knees. "Is this 'cause your dad's strict? I could meet him if you want, let him see I ain't any threat to his daughter."

"I think that would be a bad idea," I said, trying to imagine bringing a boy home to meet Dad. "But I mean…about me being complicated."

"Everybody's complicated," he said, scratching his temple.

"Not the way I am," I said. "I have a past, okay? And you really don't want to get involved with it."

"Everybody's got a past," he said. "That don't mean you can't have a future."

"Okay, but there are a lot of things you don't know about me."

"I know you're one of the prettiest girls I've ever seen," Grant said, leaning even closer. "I already know you've got a good heart. I know when we kissed I felt warm all over, like when you sit too close to a campfire, and I know no girl's made me feel that way before."

"That's really nice," I said, running fingers through my hair and looking up at the empty sky. I knew that if I looked at him, I would soften, I would give in, and I couldn't afford that. "But—"

"Listen," Grant said. I felt his hands grip mine and looked down to find his face inches away. I remembered the last time he was this close and felt my whole body flush. "I'm a big boy. I been knocked down before, and I'll be knocked down again. I can handle things that ain't simple, and I can handle things that're hard. I want you, and whatever it is about you that you think makes you so complicated couldn't make me want you less."

I opened my mouth to speak, to protest all the reasons why this was a bad idea – why it might be harder than he thought to get close to me, how it could end in both of us getting hurt – but nothing came.

"I'm gonna kiss you now," he said softly. "Is that okay?"

My head made just the slightest up-and-down motion before he brought his lips to mine and pulled my hips towards his. He had been right, I realized; it felt like sitting in front of a fire, the warmth spreading across every bit of my skin.

CHAPTER
NINE

I spent Saturday night with the girls in Layla's bedroom – which had an actual four-poster bed with sheer white drapes – trying on make-up and clothes, gossiping, and posting our most vamped-up shots to Instagram. We ended the night getting sodas at Walmart, which was the only place in town still open by then. I wondered why the girls left their make-up on, then learned the answer when we came outside and found a group of kids from our school hanging out at the edge of the parking lot, cases of beers in the backs of their pickup trucks. I didn't talk to many people, but I also didn't feel uncomfortable, and Layla made it very clear to everyone I was a member of their group. It was one of the best Saturday nights I could remember. The only way it could've been better was if Grant had been there.

I slept deep and easy once I finally got home, which

was rare for me. My phone chirped and I slowly rose from bed on stiff, creaking arms, blinking and groaning against the warm morning light. The phone chirped again. I slapped at it once, missed, and got it on the second try.

"Hello?" I croaked without bothering to check who was calling.

"Mornin', Amanda!" Anna said in a voice that was excessively cheerful, even for her.

"Mm," I groaned, stretching my back. "What's up?"

"Oh, nothin'," Anna said. "Just we're about to head to church and I thought you'd like to come." There was a strange pause, and then she quickly added, "Plus my parents wanna meet you."

"Why?" I said, as I slapped my feet on the floor. "I mean, I don't really go to church."

"Didn't you say you were Baptist?"

"Lapsed," I reminded her. "I haven't been to church since, like, middle school."

"Oh," Anna said, all her cheer gone. I paused. She didn't just sound disappointed, she sounded worried. "But that's just more reason to come, ain't it?"

"Listen, thanks for the offer," I said, "but I really don't—"

"No, Amanda," Anna whispered suddenly, "you really need to meet my parents. Like, really, really. Please?"

My stomach sank as I realized she needed me. I thought it over for a moment before saying, "Okay. I'll get dressed."

89

"Yay!" Anna said, all the cheer flooding back. "We'll be there in a half-hour."

She hung up before I could respond. I sighed and dug through my luggage. I only had one church-appropriate outfit: a pastel-pink floral short-sleeve dress with a wide purple belt that used to be Mom's, twenty-five years and ten dress sizes before. I stepped into the living room and found Dad at the kitchen table, rubbing his temples over the plate of greasy bacon in front of him. His eyes were closed and his skin was pale and blotchy.

"That's not very healthy," I said, wondering what happened to the Dad who ate salad for practically every meal.

"Hangover," he replied, his voice groaning like an old door. "Greasy food helps." He cracked his eyes and stared at me for a moment. "What's with the outfit?"

"I'm going to church," I said, leaning against the counter and checking my phone. Dad let out a hoarse laugh but cut it short when I crossed my arms and looked down.

"Oh," he said. "You were serious." He tore a strip of bacon in half and popped it in his mouth. "Sorry, it's just I can't imagine you sitting in with a bunch of holy rollers."

"My friend Anna invited me. Why can't you see me there?" I asked, though of course I knew why. I still believed in God, and for a long time my faith had been the only thing keeping me afloat. But I could never forget the day Mom had come home from seeing our pastor, red in her eyes from weeping and rage. I asked her what was wrong and heard a stream of curses, so strange in her normally sweet little voice, as she told me he'd had some *suggestions*: that I should be sent to a camp to fix me, that I should spend more time with a male role model, that I should maybe take some time away from the congregation until I found a way to fit in. We never went to church after that, though I did continue to pray.

"The text's pretty hostile to people like you," Dad finally replied, chewing slowly.

"But they don't have to know everything about me, do they?"

"Just be careful," he said. "This ain't Atlanta, and it ain't the suburbs. People around here seem nice, but you gotta be careful with who you trust."

"I know," I said flatly, feeling the scar above my ear. My phone buzzed and Anna's name appeared above a message: *we r outside*

"My ride's here. I gotta go."

"Really, though," Dad said. I turned as I was heading out the door and saw both bloodshot eyes open, a look of concern in his face. "Really. Please be careful."

I took a deep breath and nodded, feeling a sudden, shaking wave of anxiety. "I know, Dad," I said. "I will. Bye."

I hurried downstairs, where the same van Anna had

driven a few days ago stood parked outside the breezeway. I took a minute to actually read the bumper stickers this time, out of morbid curiosity: JESUS WAS A CONSERVATIVE, one read, and RIGHTS COME FROM GOD NOT GOVERNMENT; ILLEGAL ALIENS! EXACTLY WHICH PART DID YOU NOT UNDERSTAND? and I CAN'T HELP THAT I'M HOMOPHOBIC... I WAS BORN THAT WAY! I stood in place and swallowed, my mouth suddenly dry. The side door slid open and Anna leaned out, smiling.

"Whatcha waitin' for?" she said. "Hop on in." A small copy of Anna with freckles and missing teeth leaned into view and waved excitedly.

I forced a smile as I climbed in the back seat, between a pair of short blond boys in matching white short-sleeve dress shirts. Their legs were both spread so far that their knees met in the middle and neither seemed interested in moving, leaving me to clamber awkwardly over them and squeeze myself in the space left over. Something touched my butt during the manoeuvre. I made myself assume it was an accident.

A rail-thin woman with blonde hair sprayed into an updo that defied physics turned and beamed at me from the passenger seat.

"Anna, hon," she said without breaking her perfect smile, "you're being rude. Introduce me to your friend."

"Oh!" Anna said, practically jumping out of her seat. I wondered again why she was acting so strangely. "Uh,

Mom, this is my friend Amanda. Amanda, that's my mom—"

"Call me Lorraine," she bubbled, her smile still statue-perfect.

"And that's my dad."

A brick of a man grunted and gave me a brief, grudging glance in the rear-view mirror.

"This is my sister Judith," Anna said. Her sister turned and flashed me that same adorable smile and chirped, "I'm fifth grade!" I stifled a laugh and agreed that that was very impressive. Lorraine's smile faltered a little as she snapped to get Judith's attention.

"Sit down and cross your legs!" Lorraine said. Judith immediately did as she was told. There was a moment of awkward silence before Anna continued. I wondered if they could see their sons' postures in the back seat.

"And, uh, these are my brothers Simon and Matthew," Anna continued. One was a little taller than the other, and the shorter one had braces and slightly darker hair, but otherwise they could have been twins. The shorter one grunted like his dad when Anna said their names but kept his gaze locked on the window. The other just played with his phone and acted like he hadn't heard.

"Hi," I said, making myself smile pleasantly at the one who had at least bothered to grunt. He turned and made brief eye contact before dropping his eyes to my chest.

"Nice dress," he said. I started to thank him, but then

he followed with, "It makes you look like a grandma."

"Don't be a jerk to my friend, Simon!" Anna said, turning to glare at her brother.

"Watch that tone, young lady!" Lorraine said. Anna's cheeks burned red. She gave me an apologetic look and turned around again. Simon sniffed once and turned back to his phone.

"You girls have a nice time last night?" their dad said. Anna inhaled sharply and her shoulders tightened up. I looked from her back to the rear-view mirror and found her dad staring pointedly at me between glances to the road.

"Yeah," I said. "We had a lot of fun."

"Not too much, I hope."

"Why would you hope that?" I said slowly, my eyes once again darting from a paralysed Anna to her dad's unchanged stare.

"The word of the Lord is serious business," he said. "At least in our house."

"Um," I said, blinking, "of course. Yeah. My house too."

"Which verses did y'all study last night?" Lorraine said.

"I'm sorry?" I asked, confused. Anna seemed to shrink, and her dad's eyes narrowed. Then it hit me – Anna had told them we were at Bible study. "Sorry, I haven't had my coffee yet. We mostly focused on the Gospel of John."

"Ah," her dad said, nodding. " 'For the wages of sin is death.' "

I couldn't help smiling; I might not have been to church in years, but I'd paid attention when I was there. "It's definitely powerful, but that's from Romans," I said. "My favourite passage from John is, 'For God so loved the world that he gave his one and only Son, that whoever believes in him may not perish.' It's so life-focused, you know? So hopeful."

"Can't disagree," her dad said, a note of grudging respect in his voice.

"Anna, dear, you did it!" Lorraine said, clapping happily.

Anna looked up, confused. "Did what?"

"You made friends with a good influence for once."

I cleared my throat and looked out at the trees.

"Thanks," Anna whispered twenty minutes later as we sidled into a red-upholstered pew near the front. The inside of the church was small and painted stark-white, but the red carpeting and upholstery and the light pouring in through the abstract stained-glass windows made it much more beautiful than it seemed from outside. "Sorry I didn't warn you," she continued as we sat. "They were listening when I called."

"Of course," I whispered in reply, touching her wrist and smiling. "Don't worry about it."

The adults milled about in the pews, smiling and

slapping each other on the back while Anna and I sat quietly with our hands in our laps. After a few minutes, an ancient man with skin like wrinkled marble and owl eyes strode up to the pulpit, an old leather Bible tucked under his arm, and everyone grew quiet. Despite his age he moved with military grace as he silently dropped the Good Book on the lectern and flipped to the appropriate page.

"Therefore, seeing we have this ministry," the pastor said, in a huge, youthful voice that filled the church without the aid of speakers, "as we have received mercy, we faint not; But have renounced the hidden things of dishonesty, not walking in craftiness, nor handling the word of God deceitfully; but by manifestation of the truth commending ourselves to every man's conscience in the sight of God." He removed his reading glasses and looked up to survey the congregation.

"That's 2 Corinthians 4:1 and 4:2, if y'all's interested." He cleared his throat and closed his Bible, the thump resounding in the silence of the sanctuary. "Lotta good lines in Corinthians, I've always found. 'Through a glass darkly' and 'childish things' and so on, but that line I just read's got as much meat as any of the others."

My eyes drifted up to the window behind him, and the rippling grass on the hillside. Lots of the girls in the support group back home had called transitioning "living our truth", and maybe that was true. My eyes turned up just a little more and there, hanging above the window and the green grass, was a small wooden cross.

"'Fore I go any further, though, I'd like to tell a joke. Stop me if y'all've heard this'n: what's the difference 'tween a Southern Baptist and a Methodist?" A smile twitched onto his lips and he looked around expectantly, but nobody made a sound. "The Methodist says 'Hello' in a liquor store!" A few people chuckled awkwardly, but most just shifted in their seats.

"You see, we got a bit of a image problem in our church," the pastor said, growing suddenly serious. "Not that we got a *bad* image, mind; no, in fact it's the opposite: we're too *concerned* with image. We're too concerned with the external, with our appearances, with what others think of us, when we should be concerned with the internal, with our hearts, and with what God thinks of us. Radical honesty and radical faith are the heart of Christianity, ladies and gentlemen.

"I've lived that life. I've been in homes where that life is lived – perfect homes like you see on TV, full of smiling family photos and clean carpets and a cross on every wall, and it don't mean nothin'. Think of the Apostles, and what folks must've thought of 'em – a buncha dirty, ramblin', touchy-feely vagrants! But the Apostles knew they were walkin' in righteousness, and they knew so long as they were honest and true and walked with the Lord, then the Lord walked with them."

My fingers dug into my thighs and I stared at the back of the pew in front of me, feeling my heart beating. Sometimes it didn't feel like God walked with me any more. I remembered waking up in the hospital after my suicide attempt and feeling a hollow place in my heart where my faith had been. Transitioning had reawakened it a little, but it was hard to place too much hope in a God so many people said hated me.

"Radical honesty means you keep no secrets, damn the consequences. You talk about the booze, the drugs, the fornication, and the disappointments. Radical faith means you trust that the Lord visited these weaknesses and sorrows on you as part of His plan, and that as you walk with the Lord and speak honestly and demonstrate the redemption of Him others will see this, and you'll find your life enriched. A dishonest life is a life half-lived, brothers and sisters, and it's a life with one foot already in the Pit."

As the pastor went on, his words kept repeating in my brain – *a dishonest life is a life half-lived*. Was it really true? Would my friendships and relationships always be dishonest if I was forever hiding my past? My eyes scanned the crowd around me, falling on Anna's parents, so rigid-backed and attentive, and her brothers, fidgeting in their seats, before landing on Anna herself. Everyone around me, I realized, was living some kind of lie. Anna going out at night and telling her parents it was Bible study, her parents turning a blind eye to their sons' bad behaviour. Chloe and her relationship with Bee. Maybe secrets and lies were a part of life; maybe everyone had something they were lying to themselves about, or something they were hiding.

I looked up at the cross again and wondered if I was supposed to hear this particular sermon at this particular moment for a reason. I decided that the people who had said God didn't love me, who said that I didn't have a place on Earth – they were wrong. God wanted me to live, and this was the only way I knew how to survive, so this was what God wanted. This was what *I* wanted. I had chosen to live, and it seemed like, finally, I was doing just that.

CHAPTER
TEN

I sat alone at the top of the bleachers watching the football team practise. The heat was sweltering and I had to strip down to my tank top and put my blouse over the seat to keep from burning my thighs, but a pleasant breeze made it bearable. The players were hard to tell apart from this distance, but eventually I spotted Grant milling near the edge of the field, a smile on his face. He hadn't noticed me yet, but I preferred it that way. I liked seeing what he was like when I wasn't around – and I liked even more that he was so clearly at ease, so strong and graceful and confident in every small motion, so comfortable in his life in a way I'd never experienced before. Maybe, I thought, if I spent enough time around him, that feeling would rub off on me.

A squat, muscular man blew hard on a whistle and Grant hustled with the rest of the team to line up in front of a chequerboard of tyres. The coach whistled again and, two by two, the guys high-stepped across the tyres. When it was Grant's turn, he stepped up to the tyres and crouched, ready to run as soon as the whistle sounded. The coach put the whistle to his mouth and blew. Grant took off at full speed, reaching the halfway mark noticeably faster than most of his teammates. I stood, cupped my hand around my mouth, and waved the T-shirt he'd given me the night at the lake like a flag, screaming "Woo!" at the top of my lungs. Grant's face snapped up to me and he beamed. I smiled back. And then he missed a step and ate dirt just before the end of the course.

"You almost got me in trouble," Grant said, squinting against the sun as he climbed up the bleachers. He had changed into jeans and a T-shirt with a faded Captain America logo on the chest. His hair was still sopping wet from the showers, reminding me of when he emerged from the lake.

"Almost," I said, standing up and walking down a few steps to meet him. "You have to admit it was funny."

"I'm gonna be flossing out grass for a week," he said, his face splitting into a wide, boyish grin. "But yeah, it was funny."

He leaned towards me and I leaned towards him. I felt that same electric rush up and down my skin as I waited for his lips to touch down on mine. But then a loud whooping sound erupted from below us. My eyes snapped open and I stood up straight when I saw a half-dozen of Grant's teammates standing at the edge of the field, making fist-pumping motions and gyrating their hips. I felt my cheeks warm. Grant ran his fingers through his hair and tried to laugh it off.

"Sorry," he said. "My friends are jackasses."

"Just don't tell them about this," I said, surreptitiously handing him his T-shirt from the night of the party. "If an almost-kiss makes them act like howler monkeys, I imagine this would make them go nuclear."

"You're probably right," he said, stuffing the shirt in his backpack and looking over his shoulder again. He looked back at me and then gave me a quick hug, to another chorus of shouts and grunts.

"So anyway," I said, clasping my hands behind my back and looking up at a cloud of starlings as they erupted from the bleachers on the far side of the field. I looked back down at Grant. "I was wondering if maybe you wanted to come over tonight. Dad's stuck working late." His smile widened and my cheeks burned even hotter. "We could, you know, do homework and stuff."

"I'd love to do homework," he said. "And 'stuff' sounds pretty nice too."

I laughed. "Well that's good, because I kind of missed my bus so I could stay and watch you practise."

"Oh," Grant said, suddenly looking away and rubbing the back of his neck. "I just remembered, actually…" He looked down at his feet. "My car's in the shop – a buddy's giving me a ride home. So I guess I can't come over. I'm really sorry."

"I could come to your house," I offered, brushing my hair back and raising my eyebrows hopefully. "I bet my dad could get me later."

"I don't think that's a good idea," Grant said, frowning suddenly. I tried to catch his eye but he looked away. "Listen, I should go. My ride's waiting."

"Sure," I said, trying not to show my disappointment. "Text me later?"

"Definitely," he said, smiling again. He leaned up and kissed me on the cheek before muttering goodbye and jogging down the stairs.

I flopped back on the bench and stared down at the now-empty field, sighing long and loud as the cicadas' song returned. I sent out texts to Anna, Layla and Chloe, hoping at least one of them was available for a ride. A few minutes passed without a response. The sun was just starting to dip, and as the blue of the sky faded slowly to purple I pulled my phone out again and texted Virginia.

"How are things?" I typed. She responded quickly, before I could even put my phone away.

"Pretty good!" she wrote back. *"Except for the fact that I'm in line at Walmart lol. How's the new bf?"*

"*Weird*," I typed. I set the phone down on the bench and put my blouse back on against the cooling breeze. I picked up my phone again to type but realized I wanted to hear her voice. I dialled and she picked up on the first ring. "Hey," I said, realizing how much I had missed hearing her voice. She apologized as the sounds of a child throwing a fit in the checkout line assaulted my ears, but I didn't mind. It was nice to just feel her on the other end of the line.

"Anyway," she said, as the noise finally quieted down. "Tell me about you. What's up with your man?"

"Oh, I don't know," I said, feeling a little silly now. Maybe I was overreacting. I lay back lengthwise on the bench with one arm behind my head and stared up at the sky. "He acted sort of weird today. He seemed like he wanted to hang out, but then something changed and he practically ran away from me."

"So he's got some stuff going on you don't know about," Virginia said evenly. I imagined what she was doing right now: leaving Walmart and walking across the baking tarmac towards her beat-up old Bronco. I could see her getting her keys out of her expensive purse, her always-perfect, glossy fingernails as she unlocked the car door. It felt like a really long time since I had seen her. "You're keeping something pretty big from him too, aren't you?"

"I guess," I said. I almost smiled, even though I felt the total opposite – Virginia was always right. "Still. It feels different."

I sighed as a thin film of cloud scudded by overhead. Maybe I was a hypocrite, but the idea of Grant hiding something from me made my stomach turn. What if his liking me was all some elaborate trick? I knew it was a paranoid thought, but the impulse to find a dark underside to every action had been trained into me over so many years, it was hard to shake.

"You're spinning," Virginia said, always able to read my thoughts perfectly, even from the other end of the phone. "Don't jump to any conclusions. Just take your time, get to know him, figure out what his deal is. I bet it's nothing. And if it is something, you'll either bail, or you'll deal. Right?"

"Right," I agreed finally, sitting up from the bleachers and gathering my things. I would call Dad and ask for a ride and pretend nothing bad had happened. I would keep going on with my life and keep seeing Grant, and I would take things day by day. What was my big rush anyway? I knew I should want to take things slow – I should be afraid of getting close to Grant, because growing closer meant knowing things about each other, and there was so much about me that I didn't want him to know, that he could never know. But somehow, just thinking about his broad, easy grin and the way his black eyes seemed to flash in the sunlight made me feel like the only thing that mattered was being around him.

"Listen, babe, I gotta jet," Virginia said. I could hear

her car starting in the background, the radio blaring on her stereo. "You gonna be okay?"

"Yeah. Thanks for listening," I said as I began the walk down the bleachers towards the parking lot. I was starting to feel better already. "I'm think I'm going to be just fine."

CHAPTER ELEVEN

The sky was slate-grey and pregnant with the threat of another in a week of thunderstorms. A cool, moist wind rushed past Grant and me as we sat in the bed of his friend Rodney's pickup truck. I put my whipping, stinging hair in a ponytail and felt my cheeks warm when I noticed him staring at me. The truck passed over a fallen branch, bouncing both of us a few inches into the air. I clutched the raised wheel well for dear life. Grant laughed softly and smiled, then held his hands up as I kicked playfully at him.

"It's not funny!" I said, starting to smile despite myself. "Riding in the back of a truck is really dangerous!"

"It'll be worth it," he said. "Muddin's a blast, and I want you to meet the guys."

"If they're anything like Parker, I hope you won't mind me staying in the truck."

"They can be a little rough around the edges," he said, looking up the road and rubbing his neck, "but Parker's kind of a special case. You don't need to worry about him though." He turned back to me and smiled. "Really, it's less about you meeting them and more about me getting to show you off."

"Anyway!" I took my turn to look away. "Why didn't you pick me up? Isn't muddin' more fun if you have your own car?"

"So you admit it sounds like fun?" he said.

"It sounds kind of dumb," I said, shrugging apologetically.

"Well, sure it does," Grant said. "But that's what makes it fun. It's an excuse to hang out with your buddies and act like an idiot in the woods and get messy." I gave him a doubtful look. He patted his backpack. "Don't worry, though. I got picnic stuff in here. We'll make our own fun if you get bored."

"Thanks," I said as the truck turned off the highway onto a mud-and-gravel track into the woods. The canopy blotted out the already-weak sunlight and drizzled water on us for a few more minutes until the faint purr of engines could be heard; then we burst into a clearing. The grass was torn and rutted with dozens of wildly curving tyre tracks as mud-caked trucks careened back and forth with no real purpose besides the motion itself. A small crowd of equally mud-caked figures congregated around a campfire and a convoy of small red coolers. I recognized some of the faces from school, including Parker's. Grant hopped down once the truck came to a stop a way off from the crowd.

"Here you go," Rodney said as he stepped down from the cab and tossed Grant his keys. "I'm gonna grab a beer first."

"Thanks," Grant said, and climbed into the driver's seat. He looked down at me with a confused expression. "Whatcha waiting for?"

"We're going already? I was hoping for some time to digest my breakfast first."

Grant laughed. "Just one go-round, at least?" he said, lolling out the window like a defeated rag doll. "Come on, you gotta! And anyway I brought lotsa sandwiches, so if you yak we can fill you right back up."

"Charming." I laughed and made my way to the passenger seat over a chorus of conspicuously loud, whooping cries from behind us. I buckled my seat belt, enjoying Grant's nearness for a moment, until the engine roared and the truck fishtailed.

Grant leaned forward, grinning, his foot stamping the floor. The rear tyres shot great arcs of mud into the air behind us for a moment, and then we were off. I screamed and clutched his arm as the edge of the clearing rushed towards us. Grant laughed and spun the wheel at the last second, sending the truck into a long, hissing drift that splashed mud across the trunks of a dozen trees. He righted the drift and took off across the clearing again and now I was laughing too. The truck spun again, this time through a surprisingly deep depression that splattered gouts of mud on the windows and windshield. I remembered insisting that Grant explain muddin' to me and realized that he never could have, really – not in a way that would have made me understand. How much of life was like that, just waiting for me to come and give it a chance? The truck finally came to a stop at the opposite end of the clearing from our classmates. I just sat and panted for a moment, running my adrenaline-shaken hands through my hair.

"That was," I began breathily, searching for the most accurate word and failing. "That was awesome!"

"I hoped you'd like it," Grant said softly. I turned to him, grinning like a kid, and felt a flutter in my chest when I saw a much more reserved smile on his face and his dark eyes locked firmly on mine. He seemed like he was waiting for something. The flutter turned into a tightening as I realized what was about to happen.

"So," I said, looking away and stroking my hair nervously. I couldn't stop thinking about how he had darted away after school the other day. I didn't want to ruin the moment, but I needed to know. "Can I ask you a question?"

"Shoot," Grant said, leaning against the steering wheel and cocking his head.

"Are we dating?"

"Well, we're on a date."

"I know." I felt like every cell in my body was vibrating, a steady thrum from my hair to my toes. "But are we going to go on more?"

Grant frowned and looked out the windshield, and for a moment I was certain his answer was no. I was too boring. I was too stuck-up. I'd been a horrible dancer at the party and I'd assumed muddin' was stupid.

"Guess that's up to you," he said, favouring me with his full smile. I realized his front teeth were actually a little bit crooked, and I realized that a person's flaws could make them even more beautiful sometimes. "I know I want to."

"But the other day, after school, you seemed like you wanted to be as far away from me as possible."

"Shit," Grant said, sighing. His hands beat a steady rhythm on the wheel. "I'm sorry, Amanda. I guess I was just embarrassed about not being able to give you a ride. Made me feel less manly or something. It's just things with you are so fresh and new, and…you ever feel like you only want somebody to see you at your best?"

I couldn't help smiling.

"I don't just want you at your best though," I said. "I want to get to know you."

I thought about what Virginia had said, about us both keeping secrets, and I thought about my parents and how quiet it was in our home in the year before they got divorced. How they basically stopped telling each other

111

anything important. If I was going to do this, I wanted to do it right. I chewed my knuckle for a moment as I remembered the day at the plantation with Bee. "What if we played the honesty game?"

"What's that?" he said. I explained the rules the way Bee had explained them to me. Grant paused a moment, thinking. "So it's like Truth or Dare?" he said.

"Kind of." I nodded, thinking of how Bee had described it. "Just, you know, without the pervy stuff." He put on a show of pouting and I gave him a light shove. "Whatever! Play your cards right and pervy stuff might be negotiable. So you'll play it with me?"

He nodded. "Do we start now?"

I shrugged. "No time like the present, right?" I took a deep breath. "Okay, I'll go first." I took another deep breath and thought of the sermon at church with Anna. The idea of shedding all your layers of secrets and lies. Maybe someday, if we played this long enough, I would be able to tell him the truth about everything. "That night by the lake was my first kiss."

"No way," Grant said, shaking his head. "No way." I nodded emphatically. "How'd you hold out so long? Pretty as you are, guys must've been chasing you since middle school."

"Thanks," I said, blushing. "Not that I believe you, but thanks. I changed a lot last summer, so this is all pretty new," I told him truthfully. "Your turn."

"That was your first kiss," Grant said, tapping his chin and looking up at the ceiling, "but it was my best."

I touched my lips and looked down at my knees, my cheeks burning. I had been so afraid I would be a bad kisser or, worse yet, that I would kiss like a boy. I closed my eyes and remembered the kiss and my heart began to race. When I calmed down enough to look back at him I saw him blushing as well. I laced my fingers in his and said, "We can't just let that record stand, can we?"

"Why, no ma'am," Grant said, leaning towards me, "I suppose we cannot."

The kiss outside the apartment was beautiful and nervous and almost chaste. The kiss on the bleachers was tender but fleeting. What happened next was different. Our mouths connected and somehow I found myself in the driver's seat, poised above him with my hands on his hard, broad chest and my hair draped around us like a curtain. I pulled back for a moment and we just breathed, staring into each other's eyes. I felt something brush my waist and looked down to see his hand inching towards the hem of my shirt, his gaze questioning if this was okay. I bit my lip and answered by kissing his neck and biting his ear. His fingers burrowed beneath my shirt and drifted past my belly button, where they stopped for a moment, and then I felt them near my ribs.

"Hey!" Rodney yelled, pounding his fist on the window. I screamed and tumbled back to the passenger seat, banging my head in the process. "Come on, y'all, that's new upholstery!"

Grant stammered an apology as we stumbled out of the cab, both of us red-faced with embarrassment and stifled laughter. Rodney climbed into his truck in a huff and sped away, splattering both of us with mud.

We stood there in silence for a moment, shaking and smiling, until Grant leaned over and smeared some of his mud into some of my mud and the laughter we'd been holding in finally escaped in a rush.

CHAPTER
TWELVE

I sat with Bee beneath a canopy of brown and red leaves behind the art building, wisps of smoke rising from our lips as we talked. She fiddled with the settings on a new digital camera while I tried to draw her without her noticing. The cicadas had died off a few weeks before, and everything from the wind to the scratch of my pencil as it moved across the page seemed raw and loud in their absence.

"How was your report card?" I asked, my voice croaking as I handed the joint back to her.

"Shitty," she said. "I would've done okay in English if Mr Robinson didn't have it out for me, but I managed to pull out a B anyway. Got a C in chemistry and a D in calc, but who cares, right?"

"I care," I said, rolling the tension out of my neck as I turned my attention to her hair, trying to translate its movement in the breeze in frozen graphite.

"Oh yeah?" Bee said. "What do you wanna do with your life anyway?"

"I want to go to school up north," I said. "NYU maybe, if I get in. No idea what to major in though."

She leaned over suddenly and examined my drawing. I tried to hide it from her, but she grinned.

"I'm like forty pounds heavier than that, but I'm not gonna complain," she said. "Can I have that when you're done?"

"Sure," I said, turning to a new page. "But yeah, I'm not dead set on New York. I just know I want to get as far away from here as possible."

"Word," Bee said, holding the camera close to her face and screwing her nose up in concentration. "Fuck this place." She pointed the camera my way and snapped a few photos before I could turn away – a reflex from years of being unable to stomach the sight of myself in photographs. "Why a girl like you doesn't want to be seen is a mystery to me," Bee said, shaking her head. "How's that boy of yours by the way?"

"Good," I said, sketching out a bunch of random shapes that I would go back later and fill with faces. I felt my cheeks burn the way they always did when I thought of Grant. I thought of the movies we hadn't paid any attention to, and the rolled-up-jeans walks by the lake, and fingertips brushing and smiling glances in first period while Parker glared sullenly. "Great, actually. Except…"

I trailed off, unsure how much I wanted to say.

"Trouble in the garden?" Bee said, grinning. "Does he have bad breath? Is he, like, super racist?"

"No," I said slowly, arching an eyebrow. "Nothing like that. He's just… It's just…" I looked up at Bee's inquisitive face, and realized that as much as I loved talking to Virginia, I wanted to talk to someone about Grant who actually *knew* Grant, and the words began tumbling out. "He's weird sometimes. Like, we have to meet up for all our dates; he won't pick me up. He says his car is in the shop, but it's been weeks now. And he's always busy with something he doesn't want to talk about. Like, we're lucky if we get to hang out once a week, you know? No way football takes up that much of his time. I feel like he's keeping things from me."

"Maybe he's gay," Bee said. She obviously meant it as a joke, but I couldn't help imagining the worst, that he only liked me for the boyish things about me. Was it possible?

"You don't really…" I began, only to trail off. I wondered for a horrible moment if that was why he liked me, but Bee gave me a weird look and stopped my mind from swirling. "You don't really think he's gay, do you?"

"How would I know?" Bee said. "Just 'cause I'm bi doesn't mean I have magic powers. I'm not the plucky queer sidekick in your romantic comedy."

"I'm sor— Look, I didn't mean it that way," I said,

117

suppressing the urge to apologize. "It's just you kind of have dirt on everybody, don't you?"

She laughed at the look on my face. "I'm joking! Grant's straight as they come." She closed her eyes and slid down onto her back like a serpent. "Parker, though? Biggest closet case I ever saw."

"No way," I said, shaking my head. "I told you what happened at that party! He's like a giant homophobe!"

"That's how you can tell," Bee said. "You're straight, right?"

I nodded.

"How often do you think about women having sex with each other?"

I thought about it for a moment.

"Never," I said, shrugging.

"My point exactly! Homophobes think about gay sex all the time because they wanna have it. They insist being gay is a choice because every single day they have to choose not to have the kind of sex they want. Homophobes are super gay."

"I guess that makes sense," I said. "But wouldn't that make the South—"

"The gayest place in the Western hemisphere?" Bee said. "Absolutely."

We laughed at that idea for a moment, until the sound of footsteps drew our attention. We shared a quick horrified glance, and then I waved as much of our smoke away as I could while Bee stowed the joint. It was last period, but that was hardly an excuse for smoking on school grounds. We quietly sneaked around the side of the building and leaned past the corner, to see if we had heard correctly. My heart nearly stopped when I saw the front door to the art building standing open.

"Shit," Bee hissed. "Shit, shit, shit. Let's bail."

We hurried back behind the building and froze when we saw a short, middle-aged man with a slate-grey crew cut standing next to our bags holding our sketchbooks, a thoughtful expression on his square face. He looked up at us silently and raised his eyebrows.

"Bee," he said flatly. "Can't say I'm surprised. How fares your senior year?"

"Uh, great," Bee said.

"That's good," the man said, turning his attention back to our papers and sniffing conspicuously. Was he letting us know he knew we'd been smoking? "And might I know your friend's name?"

"Amanda Hardy," Bee said for me, when it was clear I wasn't going to speak.

"A pleasure, Amanda," the man said, as he tucked our notebooks under his arm. "I'm Mr Kurjak. Expect a call from me this weekend, both of you. Mind if I borrow your sketchbooks?"

"No," Bee said. I just shook my head.

"I'll get them back as soon as I can," he said, giving us

119

the vaguest hint of a nod as he turned and walked away.

Bee waited until she was sure Mr Kurjak was out of earshot and said, "That could've gone worse."

"Who was that?"

"The gym teacher."

"My life is over," I said, a sudden ringing in my ears. I breathed in panicked gulps. "I'm gonna be expelled!"

"Relax," Bee said, shouldering her backpack. "Worst-case scenario? He maybe smelled some weed. They can't kick you out over a smell."

"Are you sure?"

"Definitely," Bee said. "Probably. Maybe? It's last bell now anyway. Let's get burgers."

We had to wait until Bee sobered up enough to drive, and I was so hungry by the time we pulled into the McDonald's parking lot that I almost forgot to be anxious. Bee hopped out of the truck and strode in ahead of me. I took my time, hands in my pockets, listening to the swollen absence of the cicadas and feeling the cool touch of the fall wind on my skin. Inside, Bee was mid-conversation with a thin, prematurely balding guy behind the counter.

"What do you want?" she said, turning to me. "It's on me, since I probably ruined your Harvard plans or whatever." I opened my mouth to tell her, but a movement in the kitchen caught my eye. The cook seemed familiar to me, but his back was facing us. Just then he turned around and I saw Grant's face, grease-stained and wide-eyed, staring out at me from beneath his regulation baseball cap. His hair was lank with sweat and his shoulders sagged with fatigue. His cheeks flashed suddenly red and he broke eye contact with me after a moment.

I rushed outside and leaned against Bee's car, my heart pounding. Was *this* what Grant had been hiding from me? That he had an after-school job? Why hide that? And if it was such a big secret, what would happen now that I had seen him like this? When I saw him coming around the corner, his apron missing, my heart pounded even harder.

"Walk with me?" he said.

"Won't you get in trouble?"

"Nah," Grant said, shoving his hands in his pockets and taking off slowly down the highway. I followed him, my legs feeling clammy and rubbery. "I've covered like a million shifts for Greg. He owes me."

"Jeez," I said. "How many hours a week do you work?"

"At this job?" Grant said. "Or all of 'em together?" I raised my eyebrows and gave him a blank stare. "Yeah," he said slowly, chewing his lip. "Confession time, I guess. Let's see." His mouth moved silently and he stared at the sky as he counted his fingertips. "It's twenty hours here, ten hours doing odd jobs for Chloe's family farm in the fall and summer, and ten hours washing dishes at Hungry Dan's. So forty hours, I guess – give or take, depending on when I'm covering shifts."

"Is that legal?" I said, dumbfounded.

"Never really thought about it," he said. "I guess so now, since I'm eighteen, but probably not before then, no. Here's the only place that gives me a cheque though, so it always worked out."

"When do you find time for football?" I said. "Or parties? Or homework? Or…you know, me?"

"I don't get a lot of sleep," he said, "and I don't really do homework, a lot of the time. My grades are terrible. I cover shifts a bunch, especially in the summer. That way I can call in favours whenever a certain girl wants my attention." He winked at me and I laughed.

I reached out to touch his shoulder. "Why were you hiding all this from me?"

"I'm not a very public person in general," he said.

I nodded.

"Anyway, I'm sorry if I was weird about stuff. I just… I was afraid you'd see me differently. That and I didn't want you to feel bad about the extra shifts I work so we can go out."

"I do see you differently," I said.

He gave me an embarrassed look.

I shook my head and smiled. "I can add 'hardworking' to your list of virtues."

"Jeez," he said, with a sheepish grin. "Can this count towards the honesty game?"

"Sure," I said, "but only if this can count as mine." I hugged his arm and brought my mouth inches from his ear. "I'll probably be expelled on Monday, and I'm really, really high right now." I planted a kiss on his cheek before he could respond.

Now it was Grant's turn to laugh.

"Amanda Hardy," he said, "you might be the most interesting person I ever met."

JANUARY, SIX YEARS AGO

Their fighting woke me up at four thirty. I turned my back to my bedroom door and listened as Mom and Dad screamed at each other. Each swear word, each sharp, barking yell made me flinch as though I were being physically slapped. I stared at my reflection in my bedroom window, lined in orange by a nearby street light. I wanted to go back to sleep, but I couldn't drown out their voices.

"He's coming home with bruises once a *week* for Christ's sake!" Dad said. "We have to do *something*!"

"So you wanna throw my baby to the goddamn wolves?" Mom said, ice in her voice.

"Jesus, Bonnie," Dad said, "it's the Boy Scouts, not fucking *Oz*. The kid can't even throw a ball for Christ's sake."

It went back and forth like that. I listened but not closely, because this was an old argument. Dad wanted me to play sports, join the scouts, go camping with him and his navy buddies, do whatever it took to "toughen me up". He asked me to play catch with him once a week. The nights we didn't, he still looked disappointed, but the nights we did were in some ways worse because I had to watch the frustration grow in his eyes. He said it was for my safety, but Mom said putting me closer to the people who were bullying me would just get me bullied more, and I agreed. I had just started slipping back to sleep when their argument stopped being typical.

"I'm *not* making it about me," Dad said, a ragged edge to his voice. I opened my eyes again and rolled onto my back.

"Don't lie to yourself and don't lie to me," Mom said. "It's pathetic, and so is the way—"

"Shut up," Dad hissed.

"Do *not* tell me to shut up. And so is the way you push your issues about your manhood onto my son. You're gonna get him put in the hospital because you're afraid of your *buddies* knowin' you raised a *fairy*."

"*Shut up!*" Dad screamed. I heard glass shatter and Mom screamed in fright, and then there was a long silence. "I'm sorry," Dad said softly. "I'm so sorry."

"Get away from me," Mom said. I sat up in bed, my heart racing. This was different. Something was about to change. "I said get *away* from me!"

My door swung open quickly and the light came on as

125

Mom swooped in. Dad stood in the doorway, one hand on his hip and another in his hair, watching both of us with an expression somewhere between rage and shame. "Put your clothes on, Andrew," Mom said. "We're going on a trip."

I looked from her to Dad. He closed his eyes and took a long, slow breath. "Do what she says, bud," he said, his voice quavering. Had I ever seen Dad cry before? The idea was so strange I almost forgot what was going on. Mom tossed an *Invader Zim* hoodie and jeans onto the bed. I put them on quietly while she packed my things. Once everything was ready we walked to the door. Dad stood in the way for a second before sniffing once, loudly, and getting out of our way.

I got in the car and Mom turned it on, to ward away the cold, then went back inside for what felt like for ever before she came back out with a suitcase of her own. She threw it in the back seat and, as the sun rose, drove us both east out of the town where I was born. I would never go back.

"Where are we going?" I asked Mom once we were on I-40.

"Remember Grandma and Grandpa?" she said, a twitching half smile spreading across her face. It didn't reach her bloodshot eyes.

"Yes," I said, though I didn't remember them well. They lived in Atlanta and we almost never had time to visit them.

"We're gonna stay with them for a while," Mom said, her voice trembling. "Like a vacation." We were both quiet for about an hour, and then as we got close to Nashville, Mom spoke again. "How much did you hear?"

"Of what?" I said.

"The fight."

"Oh," I said, shrugging and looking out my own window. My throat felt dry. "Not much. I only just woke up when you came in my room. Was it a bad one?"

"Don't you worry about it," Mom said, and now it sounded like she was gagging. "All I ever, *ever* want you to worry about is doin' good in school and bein' yourself. Okay?"

"Okay," I said. I doubted she would actually accept what "myself" really entailed, but I loved her all the same for saying it. I smiled at her. Her eyes were pinched almost shut and her whole face was collapsing with the need to cry. I put my left hand in her right and leaned against her while she drove.

CHAPTER
THIRTEEN

On the screen in front of us, Nino Quincampoix slipped a note under Amélie Poulain's door. I put a hand on Grant's knee. His eyebrows were furrowed, apparently too caught up in reading the subtitles to take the hint. He put an arm around my shoulder and pulled me close. I rested my head on his shoulder, breathing him in.

"Wait," Grant said, as Amélie pressed Play on a VHS tape she found in her apartment and an old man's face appeared on her screen, exhorting her to live in the moment and enjoy her life instead of keeping herself distant from other people. "Who's that guy?"

"Mr Dufayel," I said, nuzzling him. "Amélie's downstairs neighbour, remember?"

"The grocery-stand guy?" Grant frowned.

"The one who does the paintings," I said. "With the bone thing."

"Oh!" Grant said, but by the time he got it the video was over and the scene was moving on. "Could we rewind it?" he said. "Sorry."

"You don't have to apologize," I said, and rewound it for him. He absorbed the scene this time, though it took all of his concentration. He gasped as Amélie ran to her door and opened it to find Nino, and I giggled. He hugged me even tighter as she brought Nino into her apartment and they faced each other, really, for the first time. He kissed me just above my ear as their kiss ended and Amélie and Nino were seen on Nino's bike riding up and down the streets of Paris together. He didn't know he was kissing me on my scar, but I felt the line of numbness where the stitches had been and shivered.

"So," I said, pulling away from him playfully, "what did you think?"

"I liked it," Grant said slowly. "I don't think I understood it, but I liked it."

I turned and draped my legs across his lap. I loved my legs – they were the only part of my body that had felt feminine all along. Grant must have liked them too, because he bit his lip and smiled.

"Thanks for coming over. I needed a little distraction after gym-gate." I sighed.

As promised, Mr Kurjak had called Bee and me at home over the weekend to tell us what would happen now that we'd been caught without a teacher after a full quarter of school. While we were chastised for not reporting it much sooner, the fact that we'd actually used the time to work on art had in fact counted for something, and we weren't in trouble. We were, however, enrolled in gym, starting on Monday.

"You're very welcome," he replied with a grin. "Damsel in distress and all."

I rubbed my toes against his biceps and stretched. "My dad's not home till ten," I said.

Grant pushed his hand through his hair and looked up at the ceiling. "I don't wanna make a bad impression on him."

"Don't worry about it," I said. "He has a total fetish for schedules. He's practically a robot. He'll never even know you were here."

"How long has your dad lived here anyway?" Grant said, his hand on my calf.

"About six years," I said. "Why?"

"Oh, I guess I was just thinking it's funny I've never seen you before," he said. "Here, let's clean up." He gingerly moved my leg and picked our dishes up off the coffee table.

"I'd never been here before," I said, sighing as I walked to the sink to rinse the dishes. "My dad and I…we didn't talk for a while after the divorce." I stared out the window at the spot where the sun turned the whole sky purple as it sank past the Appalachians. "This is the first time we've seen each other since Mom and me left."

"How come?" Grant said, loading the dishes into the washer as I handed them to him. "Were you mad at him?"

"Kind of," I said. I wanted to change the subject, but there were some things I'd wanted to talk about for years that I'd only ever plastered in chat boxes to strangers on the internet, and now I wanted to say them out loud. "But it was more than that. In a way...I was the reason my parents got divorced."

"Really?" Grant said. A dozen internet friends and support-group members had reassured me that it wasn't my fault, that divorce was never the child's fault, and I had hated them for it. "That sucks."

I sighed. "You're the first person who didn't just feed me a platitude when I told them that," I said. "Thank you."

"No problem," he said, shrugging. "Sometimes bad stuff happens that a few nice words can't fix. I get it." He reached out for my hand. "But if you don't mind me askin', how exactly do you think you made 'em divorce?"

"I had a problem when I was a kid," I said, feeling my throat start to close. I felt like a liar again. "Raising me was so hard that my parents were stressed out all the time, and they disagreed on basically everything about how to help me." I took a deep breath and dried my hands before taking his. "I've seen their wedding photos, though, and I've looked through old albums. They were happy before I was born, and then they weren't."

"Damn," Grant said. "That's rough. You know just because you may be the reason for it, that doesn't mean it's your fault, right?"

"I forget sometimes," I said, squeezing his hand. "Thanks for reminding me. That's why I came here actually: I needed a fresh start."

The room grew quiet. Grant was staring at me, clearly thinking very hard about something. I tapped my foot, afraid of what those thoughts might be. "I've been talking so much, but you haven't told me about your family. Are your parents still together?"

"Sorta," Grant muttered, his mouth stretching into a flat line. "Listen, my family ain't very interesting."

"Come on," I prodded. "You can talk to me." I flashed him a teasing grin and drew closer. "If you want, we can count it as one of your secrets."

"We don't have to play this stupid game though," Grant said, rubbing the bridge of his nose. "Everything doesn't have to be all deep and dramatic. Don't you just wanna talk about normal stuff and have fun?"

"I do," I said. I reached out to take his arm. "Look, I'm sorry."

"It's okay," Grant said, pulling me into a weak hug and shaking his head. "I'm just not ready to talk about family stuff, all right?"

"Why not, though?" I said, looking up and brushing a strand of black hair out of his eyes. "Don't you trust me?"

"It's not that, just – why can't you leave it alone?" He stood up.

I stood and took a step towards him just as a key turned in the lock. We both froze, eyes wide, as Dad walked in looking tired and grumpy, his tie already loosened.

"Hello," Dad said, his voice cold as he shut the door behind him.

"Hi, Dad," I said, my eyes darting from him to Grant and back again.

"Hi," Grant said, holding out his hand for a shake. Dad looked at the hand and then looked at me.

"Are you going to introduce us?" he said.

"Right!" I said. "Dad, this is my…friend, Grant. Grant, this is Dad."

"Grant," Dad said, finally reaching out and giving him two firm shakes before turning to set his briefcase on the kitchen table.

"I'll, uh," Grant said, zipping up his hoodie and giving me an awkward look as he backed towards the door. "I was just, you know, on my way out."

"Okay, yeah," I said, mouthing the word "sorry" while my back was turned to Dad.

"Drive safe," Dad said.

When the door closed he turned towards me, a grim look on his face. "I would appreciate an explanation."

"You said I could have a friend over," I said, shrugging and avoiding eye contact. I knew how lame it sounded, but a part of me felt indignant too, that he was standing there, judging me, caring how I spent my time and setting rules for me for the first time in over six years.

"Don't be coy," he said, moving towards the cabinet where he kept the liquor and removing a bottle of whiskey. He got down a glass and took a sip without flinching. "You know I didn't mean you could have a boy over."

"I guess I know now," I said, walking past him to my bedroom door. The words hung there in the silence, challenging, but I didn't want to have this fight right now, not after the way I'd left things with Grant. "I'm tired. Goodnight."

"Wait," he said, stepping towards me, but the door was between us before he could say anything more.

CHAPTER
FOURTEEN

The locker room smelled of mildew and bleach. The fluorescent lights buzzed angrily, but a decades-old brown film on the panels dimmed their light. I remembered all the times boys at my old school had cornered me out of the sight of a teacher and hit and kicked me in places that couldn't be seen through my clothes. I remembered them yelling, "Faggot!" and laughing. I remembered how I was certain teachers knew what was happening and how they did nothing. I remembered the boys warning that nobody would care if I said anything anyways, and if I ever did get them in trouble they would put me in the hospital.

I stood there, frozen in the doorway. Two dozen girls dropped their conversations and looked up at me. I cleared my throat and shifted my weight from foot to foot for a painful moment, before Layla appeared, grabbing my hand and leading me to her locker. The other girls' attention slowly drifted back to their own business.

I tried to control my breathing and kept walking, following Layla's footsteps gratefully.

"What are you doing here?" Layla said as we reached her locker. "Was art cancelled today?"

"For ever, actually," I said, chewing my fingernails. "When they found out we hadn't had a teacher all semester, the school put me here. Not sure what they'll do with Bee. I think they were afraid if they put us both in the same class again we'd cause more trouble."

"Reasonable fear," Layla said with a smile as she pulled her knitted sweater over her head. Instinctively I looked away, remembering the way the girl from school had screamed when she'd seen me in the women's room, and how angry her father had been at the idea of finding me there. "You okay?" Layla said, looking concerned. "That's an awfully serious expression."

"Fine," I said, shaking my head and returning to chewing my nails. "I'm fine. Just thinking about something."

"Grant, probably," she said, poking me with her elbow. "He came over Friday, right?"

"Yeah," I said, fiddling with the buttons on my blouse. My head was already buzzing so I focused on those buttons, trying to get them under my control. How silly it was that I still had trouble with them. Why did boys' and girls' buttons have to face different directions? "My dad got home early though, so…"

"Woof!" Layla laughed. "He didn't catch you…doing stuff, did he?"

"No, thank God," I said. I hadn't been able to stop thinking about that night, and how awkward Grant's departure had been. Thankfully he texted as soon as he got home, apologizing for an evening cut short and promising another date soon, but things still felt tense.

I sat down on the bench. I had reached the final button on my blouse. I wouldn't be able to stall much longer.

"You okay?" Layla said.

"I'm good," I said shakily. There was no way she believed me, but she smiled and pretended to. She finished dressing and sat down to lace her shoes, though I noticed she was doing it over and over to stay with me.

I took a deep breath, closed my eyes, and shrugged off my shirt. A few seconds passed, and I opened my eyes to find Layla looking at my chest with raised eyebrows.

"You know we're running today, right?" she said.

"So?" I said, looking down at the padded bra I'd been wearing since I started hormones.

"Late bloomer?" she said, standing and giving me an understanding smile. I half-smiled and nodded, wondering what I'd got wrong this time. "And you said you live with your dad, so it makes sense there's stuff you don't know." She looked around and saw the locker room was quickly emptying, and proceeded in a lower voice. "Your boobs are too big to run in that. Today is going to *hurt* for you."

"They are?" I said. The idea had never occurred to me.

"There are worse problems to have," she said, poking her tongue out and winking at me. "Just get a sports bra and you'll be fine."

"Thanks," I said, blushing for what felt like the millionth time since I moved here. I wondered when I'd reach the end of things I didn't know.

I trudged out to the parking lot after school, my chest aching from an hour of running. I had taken my time afterwards, and by the time I reached the parking lot, the buses were leaving without me.

I was too tired to be upset. Thankfully the weather was cooler than the last time I'd been stranded. I squatted on the steps, closed my eyes, and ran my fingers through my sweat-drenched hair. Layla had a car, and she probably wasn't too far away yet. But I felt like I owed it to Dad to try him first after what happened last time, so I texted to ask him for a ride. To my surprise he replied almost immediately, saying he would be right over. I rested my face in my hands and slipped into an exhausted daze, only looking up at the sound of Bee's voice.

"You look like shit," she said, shouldering her bag and leaning against the railing next to me.

"I feel worse," I said, rubbing my temples. "Just got out of gym."

"Ah," Bee said, her face screwing up like she just ate something sour. "They got me in first block. Had to shift some other classes around, but they really don't want us hoodlums together on school grounds."

"I'm a hoodlum now?" I said. She laughed and patted me on the shoulder in a "welcome to the club" sort of way. "How was gym for you?"

"I cut class," she said, squaring her shoulders and looking suddenly distant. I started to lecture her but she cut in before I could. "I know. I'm already on thin ice." She pursed her lips and took a deep breath. "It's just, the last thing I need is to run around in short-shorts while the Neanderthals make comments and the teacher pretends not to hear." I gave her a questioning look, surprised to hear Bee admitting that what people said bothered her, and she stiffened even more. "I gotta go, actually. You need a ride?"

"My dad's coming," I said.

" 'Kay. See ya," she said, waving and hustling away. I stared after her, wondering how Bee had become the person she was, lost in thought until Dad's car pulled up.

"Thanks for picking me up," I said. I melted into the passenger seat and heaved a heavy sigh of exhaustion.

"Happy to," he said, arching an eyebrow at my show of pain. "Everything okay?"

"Yeah," I said, leaning back and sighing at how comfortable the seat was. Every part of me ached. "Actually, could we swing by Walmart on the way home?"

"What for?"

"Nothing," I said, too embarrassed to tell him what I needed to buy. To my surprise, he smiled.

"She used to do that," he said, shaking his head. Your mom, I mean. I think y'all are confused about what that word means, like maybe you got it mixed up with 'everything'?"

"Yeah," I said, smiling at Dad even though it felt a little strange to think about acting like either of my parents. "I guess you're right. Sorry for being weird." I took a deep breath. "I need a new bra." I thought of Grant seeing me in the ratty old thing currently stuffed in my backpack and corrected myself. "Bras. I need new bras."

"I see," he said, instantly stiffening. His hands squeezed the wheel. "Look, we need to talk about the other night."

"Yeah?" I said, stiffening in return.

"You need to be more careful," he said. "Especially with boys."

"I thought I was," I replied, though I knew that was far from the truth. I had promised him I was coming here to study and graduate, to be safe. I wasn't sure what I was doing with Grant, but it certainly didn't fit into that plan.

"Christ," Dad said. I turned to see him squeezing the

bridge of his nose. "I thought you took this seriously. I really did."

"How am I not taking things seriously?" I said, my anger from the other night rushing back.

"You were always such a timid kid," he said, shaking his head. "Always hovering around your mother's legs with that serious expression. You used to hate doing anything even a little dangerous."

"I still do," I said.

"Then why are you going to church with fundamentalists?" he snapped, turning a hard glare on me. I flinched. "Why are you having boys alone – and not just boys, mind you, but athletes by the look of that Grant character—" He took a deep breath and lowered his volume, but the edge was still there. "I trusted you to keep your head down."

I felt hot tears coming, but I blinked them away. I watched my reflection in the car window, beyond it trees and dusty road passing in a blur. "I just want to have a normal life."

"And I just want you to live past your senior year," Dad said, his jaw clenched. He let out a long breath. "People like you get killed by people like him."

"Grant's not like that," I said, my voice sounding tinny and distant.

"He's a teenage boy," Dad said, raising his voice again. "They're all like that! You don't understand this at all, do you? God, I still remember that letter you sent when you started your hormone pills, where you told me you'd been a girl all along. I hadn't understood it then but now I think I do, because you're acting like a girl now. You're acting like a little girl who's so love-struck she's lost her mind."

I closed my eyes and took deep, even breaths. "I'll be more careful," I said, my voice low.

"You'd better," he said, glaring out the windshield. "One wrong move and I'm sending you back to your mother."

He pulled into the Walmart parking lot and the car came to a stop. I slammed my door and didn't look back as I strode across the asphalt. I wasn't sure who I was angrier with – him for trying to control me, or myself for arguing, when a part of me still suspected he was right.

CHAPTER
FIFTEEN

Friday night came as slow as torture, but it finally came. All week I had been thinking about what Dad had said in the car, that I shouldn't be with Grant, that I was being foolish. But when Grant told me he wanted to take me somewhere on Friday night, I couldn't help myself. I said yes.

I waited on the bottom step of the apartment's breezeway when Grant arrived in a sedan older than me, its front left panel powder blue while the rest was varying degrees of rust red. The engine rattled like a maraca, and though the light was dim I could see the upholstery sagging inside. Grant stepped out, hands in his pockets and eyes cast to the ground. I walked over and smiled.

"How do you find yourself this evening, m'lord?" I said, trying to defuse the tension, but he didn't smile. He bit his lip and shuffled for a quiet moment before giving me an anxious look. "We don't have to go," he said. "We could walk somewhere."

"Why would we do that?" I said, circling slowly to his side of the car.

"Because my car's a piece of junk," he said. "It's so embarrassing."

"She'll make point five past light speed," I said, patting the hood of his car and doing my best Han Solo impression. "She may not look like much, but she's got it where it counts, kid." I leaned up, kissed him softly on the lips, and grinned, arching an eyebrow. "I've made some…*special* modifications myself."

He smiled a little, but something was obviously still on his mind. I was starting to lose hope when he said, "Okay, well, get in the car you stuck-up, half-witted, scruffy-looking nerf herder."

"Who's scruffy-lookin'?" I asked in mock indignation as I hopped into the car. The seat screeched and tilted as I sat in it, and I realized when I reached that there was no seat belt. Grant sat down and started the poor, limping engine and we headed out.

"Hey, wait," he said, frowning. "How come you're Han and I'm Leia? Shouldn't it be the other way around?"

"You were pouting," I said, matter-of-factly. "Han Solo doesn't pout. You can have your Han privileges back when you cheer up. Can I ask what's on your mind?"

"You can," Grant said, scratching his temple and

frowning again. "You'll find out soon enough."

"Where are you taking me?"

"That's a surprise. Hopefully a good one."

I swallowed dryly and gripped the door handle, my own anxiety building the further I got from home. The car rattled even worse once it hit speed on the highway, to the point that I was afraid it was going to come apart.

"Sorry again about the other night," I said, twisting a strand of hair.

"You don't need to apologize," he said, shaking his head. "I wouldn't be so happy either if I had a daughter and found her in my house alone with a boy."

"No," I said, "I mean about pushing you too hard to talk about your family."

"Oh," Grant said. "That. I mean, I should be glad you want to know that kind of stuff. I should be really, really glad you're interested in that. And I'm trying."

He turned off the interstate onto a highway miles outside of town. The street lights grew thinner and thinner until he eventually turned onto a dirt road and the only light remaining was his car's one functioning headlight.

We pulled into a patch of gravel beside a brown double-wide trailer. A light came on above the trailer's tiny latticed porch, revealing a pair of bony, tired-looking dogs chained near a garden where a dozen chickens hopped around angrily at the sudden disturbance before fleeing behind the trailer to escape the light.

Grant turned to me and grimaced a little. He let out a long, slow whistle. "This is my mom's car. It was never in the shop. I just didn't want you to see it, just like I didn't want you to see where I live." He took a deep breath and turned to me. "You sure you wanna come inside?"

I squeezed his hand and kissed his cheek. "I would love to meet your family."

I followed him as he walked up to the porch, giving the chained-up dogs a wide berth. The screen door swung open and two girls hopped out, one with long black hair in overalls, who couldn't have been more than eight and a brown-haired girl in a tank top, who looked a little older. They ran up to us, cackling happily.

"Is this her?" the older one asked.

"Yeah," Grant said, kneeling to give both girls hugs.

"You're really tall!" the younger one said, yanking on her hair and looking up at me with the same big, black eyes that stared out at me from Grant's face. "How'd ya get so tall?"

"It kind of just happened," I said with a shrug.

"Ignore her," Grant said, smiling and tousling the girl's hair. She screamed in delight and jumped away, grinning with a mouth missing a third of its teeth. "That's my baby sister Avery."

"Hi," I said. She giggled again and ran inside. I saw the way Grant watched her, almost like a parent, and felt something soften in my chest.

"I'm Harper," the older girl said. "Grant ain't stopped talkin' about ya for weeks."

"I hope I don't disappoint!" I said.

"Ya better not," she said, putting her hands on her hips. "Anybody messes my brother around'll get a ass whuppin'."

"Jesus, Harper, get inside!" Grant said, pointing at the door and giving her a stern expression. She stuck her tongue out and followed her sister.

"Sorry," he said to me with a sigh as his shoulders sagged. "We don't have company a lot."

"It's fine," I said, hooking my arm around his and smiling. "They're adorable. I'm ready to go in when you are."

"Gotta get it over with, I guess," Grant said, and we walked inside.

Grant's trailer was the exact opposite of Dad's apartment. Where Dad's walls were white because he had trouble understanding the point of colour, this living room's walls practically glowed in lime green and purple. Where Dad's furniture was brown because that seemed like the easiest way to keep it looking clean, none of this room's furniture matched and the upholstery's colours ranged across the whole spectrum. Where Dad's walls and tables were bare of any decoration, this room's walls were almost completely hidden behind dozens of family photos and strange, psychedelic portraits of a Jesus who looked nothing like the sterile image worshipped at Anna's church.

A thin, grey-haired woman with a heavily lined face leaned out from the kitchen and waved.

"Hey, sugar!" she said in the gravelly voice of a heavy smoker. "Is this her? Oh my lord, Grant! She's so pretty I could just die." I covered my face. "I'm Grant's mama, but you can call me Ruby. I'd come give y'all proper hugs but –" she gestured to her white, flour-caked hands and forearms – "I got some washin' up to do before dinner. Grant, hon, can you make sure your sisters're decent for company?"

"They aren't," Grant said. "I'll go get 'em ready. Amanda, you wanna come with? I can give you the tour." He gestured to the rest of the trailer with a sweep of his arm, a sarcastic look on his face. I shook my head.

"Actually, mind pointing me to the ladies'?"

"Sure," he said, then pointed at the closest door in the hallway leading to the bedrooms. "Bathroom's over there."

The bathroom was tiny and decorated in the same bizarre style as the living room. My eyes landed on a cluster of pill bottles on the sink: Seroquel, 800mg, for Ruby Everett. When I was in the mental hospital after my suicide attempt, one of the other patients had been on that medication for delusions and hallucinations. I knew Grant's home life was hard, considering how much he had to work, but now I wondered how much worse it was than I had thought.

As I stepped out of the bathroom I peeked into the room beyond. It was small, with a well-made twin bed, a battered-looking acoustic guitar on a stand, a poster of the Vols and a small television on a desk next to a pile of DVDs. A stack of glossy paperbacks stood on the floor. I picked one up and immediately recognized the *Sandman* series. A page was dog-eared near the beginning of volume two.

"Hey," Grant said from behind me. I turned, afraid he was going to be angry at me for snooping, but he smiled. "Dinner's ready."

"Thank you," I said, walking to him slowly, "for bringing me here."

"No problem," Grant said, shrugging. "Just…I'm sorry in advance if dinner's weird."

"I can handle weird," I said as we walked out to the kitchen table. Grant gave me a worried look as we sat down at a table covered in a faded green-apple tablecloth with red-apple place mats. The room was decorated with green-apple wallpaper and stickers of apples covered the refrigerator. Plates of collard greens, fried okra, cornbread and fried catfish steamed as they waited for us to dig in. I grabbed my fork, but Grant touched my arm and slightly shook his head. I started to ask why when Ruby began to say grace.

"Give us, O God, the nourishing meal, well-being to the body, the frame of the soul," she began, in the low voice of someone reciting poetry. I lowered my utensils and closed my eyes, feeling a tingle at the back of my neck. "Give us, O God, the honey-sweet milk, the sap and the savour of the fragrant farms."

"That was beautiful," I said, staring at Ruby. "Is that from the Bible?"

"Don't know where it's from. Mama used to say it, and her mama used to say it, so that's what we say."

"Well, I think it's stupid," Avery said. Grant opened his mouth angrily to chastise her, but Ruby beat him to the punch.

"Now, Avery," Ruby said, "you know Jesus loves you like you love them dogs and all them chickens and all the birds in the woods. And you love them a lot, don't you?" Avery nodded. "And lovin' them like you do, wouldn't it just hurt your heart to reach out to try and comfort one of those little babies and they scratched your finger?" Avery thought and then nodded more slowly. "Well, that's what it's like for Jesus when you say things like that." Avery's eyes widened. "You don't wanna hurt Jesus, do you?"

"No…" Avery said, looking down at her plate. I stared and thought of Dad and all the times he had yelled at me as a kid. For a moment I wished someone had spoken to me like Ruby.

"This all looks so delicious," I said, picking up my fork again.

"It ain't nothin'," Ruby said, waving a hand at me and smiling.

"No, really!" I said. "I haven't had a meal like this since I moved here. Dad's not much of a cook."

"You ain't from here?" Harper said with a mouth full of cornbread, spraying crumbs across the tablecloth.

"I'm from Tennessee originally," I said between bites. "But out west near Memphis. Little town about an hour north called Jackson. Then my parents split up and me and Mom settled down just outside Atlanta and Dad moved here."

"Well, then why'd you come to this shithole if you could've stayed someplace like that?" Harper asked.

"Don't swear at the damn table!" Grant said, rubbing his temple.

"You just swore!" Harper said, banging the table for emphasis.

"Damn! Damn! Damn!" Avery said, giggling and bouncing. Ruby apologized to me, but I could tell she was fading quickly.

"My dad lives here, and I hadn't seen him in a while," I said. They talked over me. "Atlanta's not all that great," I added, hoping to cut through the conversation. Harper and Grant both gave me a confused look, while Avery's attention drifted from swearing to poking her food into interesting shapes. "I don't know. Maybe it is for some people. It wasn't for me." I glanced at Grant and squeezed his hand.

"It's nice that you live with your daddy," Avery said suddenly, looking at me wistfully. "I miss my daddy."

Ruby, Harper and Grant all froze, giving one another a strange look. Grant cleared his throat and silently began clearing plates.

"Avery, shug," Ruby said, slurring just a little. "Why don't you go play?"

"Okay, Mama," Avery said, hopping down from her chair and flopping down near a pile of naked, half-bald Barbie dolls.

"You gonna help or just sit there?" Grant said, poking his head out of the kitchen to glare at Harper. She stuck her tongue out at him and stalked off towards her bedroom.

"Don't mind her," Ruby said softly. Her eyes were half-lidded and unfocused. "She always gets upset when people talk about her daddy."

"Oh," I said, as I stood and gathered the few remaining plates to help Grant. We hand-washed dishes in silence, him staring off into the distance and me afraid to ask what was going on.

"You ready to go?" he said as he placed the last of the plates in the drying rack.

"Yeah," I said, and Grant gave me a quick grin.

He kissed his mom on the cheek and headed outside.

"Thanks for dinner," I said as I picked up my purse. Her eyes fluttered like she was just waking up and she pulled me into a hug. I stiffened at first but quickly hugged her back. She smelled like cigarettes and mint and lemons.

"Thank you," she said.

"What for?"

"For making my boy smile."

CHAPTER
SIXTEEN

I held Grant's hand as we pulled out onto the main road. He squeezed mine in return, though his grip seemed weaker than usual. He didn't say anything, and I didn't want to press him, but eventually the rattling of the engine started to get to me.

"Grant." I put a hand over his and leaned over, lightly kissing his cheek. "We're near the lake. Pull over."

I used the light on my phone to find a small path and, taking his hand, led him into the woods towards the tree house where we had gone after that first party. I remembered every step of the path; I had thought of that night so many times that I could have made my way to the lake in my sleep. Grant was distracted, or nervous, or both, so he followed my lead. We reached the old tree house and climbed up wordlessly. The lake was as beautiful as last time, though a cold wind whipped across its surface, sending my hair swirling. Grant touched the back of my arm, and suddenly I felt very warm.

"You're the first person I ever brought home," he said, pulling me closer. I breathed in sharply and felt a pressure building near the bottom of my stomach. I realized I was shaking. "I've been too embarrassed to bring anybody over since we moved into the trailer."

"Thank you for trusting me," I said. The silence swelled between us.

"When I was fifteen," I began, feeling like I should tell him about my suicide attempt, like I should trade one of my secrets for his, but he kissed me before I could go any further. Our kiss started innocently enough, just lips pressed together like a dozen times in the past, but then his lips parted and mine parted, and our lips moved like we were whispering silent secrets into each other's mouths. I felt the tip of his tongue brush my teeth, and then our tongues were touching, and I heard myself whimper without meaning to do it. My knees failed and we lowered ourselves to a kneel, our fingers laced and our mouths never parting.

His fingers brushed the bottom of my stomach. I wanted them there, but years of terror made me brush his hand away. After a moment, I gently took his wrist and put his fingers back where they had been. His hand moved up further, and then he had the hem of my shirt in both hands, and he was lifting it. I broke our kiss and scuttled backwards, breathing heavily and trying to pick just one out of the swirl of feelings fighting to break the surface. I closed my eyes and tossed my shirt aside with trembling hands. We came together again and his hands were everywhere, on my back and sides and stomach and tracing my ribs. He reached behind me and, without breaking the kiss, started to unclasp my bra. Instinctively I backed away again, leaving my bra clasped.

"Can we slow down?" I said, wrapping my arms around myself.

"Of course," Grant said, quickly handing me my shirt. I pulled it over my head and saw him smiling gently once I had it on. "Of course we can."

"Can we...is it okay if we cuddle?" I said, brushing my hair back. "I didn't get touched much before I met you." I didn't finish the rest of the thought: *and I didn't think I ever would*. "I kind of need to – to ease into the idea of it."

"I think we can manage that," Grant said, wrapping his arm around me and pulling me in so I was lying on my side using his arm as a pillow. I kissed his cheek and we both turned to look at the stars. They were even more visible in the crisp fall air than they had been in the summer. I could even see the Milky Way, a band of white smeared across the night sky.

"I saw you're reading *Sandman*," I said. "I would have loaned you my copies."

"I actually got it before we started dating," he said. "I thought if I read the books you liked it might impress you."

"That's sweet," I said, closing my eyes and nuzzling deeper into his arms. "You know I was already into you, right?"

"I didn't at the time," he said, pulling me in tighter. "You acted like I was a serial killer at first."

"Things were hard at my old school," I said, bringing my face closer to his again.

"I figured, from some things you'd said." Grant nodded. "You wanna talk about it?"

"I don't know," I said. "I think so, but maybe not right now."

"That's okay," Grant told me, and we were quiet until he started talking again. "I don't know where Dad told Mama he was workin'. I don't know if she even remembers any more, but I remember it was a real job, and I remember the day we found out he didn't have it. The police showed up at our house, back when we had a house in town, and they had papers from the judge. It turned out he'd been going out in the woods to an RV with some buddies and cookin' meth for years.

"Avery wasn't even a year old when this happened. Mama had three kids and no income. We moved in with my grandma for a little bit, but then Mama had what the doctors called a psychotic break from all the stress, and apparently she said some things Grandma still ain't forgiven. Mom's medicine made her better, but she can't really work on it, so—"

"So you're the only thing keeping your family afloat," I said.

He nodded. "All I ever wanted was to keep Mama outta the loony bin and my sisters outta foster care, and that kept me so busy I couldn't give much thought to anything else. But being around you makes me feel...different. Like anything's possible. It's almost scary, you know? It feels selfish to say it but I've been wanting more and more to leave my family behind and just...go wherever I want, be whatever I want."

"Yeah," I said. "I've spent my whole life thinking about how I'm going to get away. Head up north, disappear in some big city like New York or Boston. Maybe if I'm lucky, live in Paris."

"Oh," Grant said, rolling onto his back again. "I didn't know that."

"Yeah," I said. "I'm going to apply to NYU. I think I'll get in. It's weird though. It's what I've wanted for so long, but it's scary too. It's scary to think of leaving here, of being so far from my parents and everything I know. But then it's the only way I can be really free, that I can finally live somewhere that people understand me."

"What's that supposed to mean?" he said, frowning and sitting up. I cocked my head and looked up at him, feeling a sudden lurch in my stomach.

"Just that there are things about me that not everyone can understand," I said, realizing my mistake even as the words were coming out.

"What am I to you?" he said, turning to look at the lake, his nostrils flaring.

"You're my boyfriend," I said, rising to a kneel and wrapping my arms around him from behind.

"For now," he said, stiffening at my touch. "Until you find somebody at your fancy college who doesn't have trouble understanding movies and gets the weird books you like."

"Grant," I said, kissing the back of his neck. "I like you, all right?"

"But you don't think I can understand you," he said.

"It's complicated," I said, turning his head to face me. His eyes darted away but I kissed him, holding him still. "I like you more than anyone I've ever met. It's just – there are things that are really hard to say." Grant stared at me, his eyes boring into mine, and I felt naked right then, like he could see everything, the things I wanted him to know and the ones I didn't too.

"You can tell me anything, Amanda, you know that. Haven't I shown you that?"

I buried my face in his neck and breathed him in again. I thought about what he had said, that I could tell him anything, and I knew that he was right – or at least that he thought he was. But until the moment he learned

159

the truth, I couldn't know how he would feel, and that was a risk I wasn't ready to take. "I'll try, okay? You deserve that. I promise I'll try."

CHAPTER
SEVENTEEN

I pressed my forehead against the window as Layla's car pulled north onto I-75. I could just make out Chloe to my right, her reflection ghostly against the mountains on the horizon. She sat with her shoulders slumped and a hollow look in her eyes. She didn't seem interested in talking.

"Where are we going again?" I said, my breath fogging the glass. I glanced at the phone in my lap and saw a new text from Grant: *Sorry about last night.* I had wanted to see him today, to try to smooth things over from last night, but the girls showed up around lunchtime, honking the car horn loudly, claiming they were staging an intervention: I was addicted to my boyfriend, and it had to stop.

"Maze of the Damned!" Anna and Layla both yelled in their spookiest voices.

"So, what, like a haunted house?" I said, as I typed out a response to Grant: *Don't apologize! I'm glad we talked. I miss you.*

"No," Anna said, "a haunted corn maze just south of Knoxville. So it's a maze but it's also 'maize', get it?"

I rolled my eyes but I was smiling.

"You'll really like it," Layla said, flourishing her free hand like a claw and deepening her voice. "It's a macabre feast for every sense!"

"Also," Anna said, bouncing, "there's funnel cake!"

Anna and Layla spent the hour-long trip giggling with each other over snippets of gossip, bickering over something sacrilegious Layla said, and singing along loudly to Taylor Swift. I didn't know the words so I made up my own, which sent the girls into hysterics – except Chloe, whose silence was as loud as an air horn. It took Grant most of the ride to respond, but eventually I got another text: *I miss you too.*

We headed to the Maze of the Damned just as the sun finished creeping out of sight. We walked past a looming grain silo, a red-roofed barn with SEE ROCK CITY painted on it in white text just visible in the light from a nearby bonfire, and a dark-windowed farmhouse that looked at least a hundred years old. On the other side lay rolling fields dotted with patches of orange firelight, and in the centre, rising like the walls of a fortress, was the corn maze itself.

Nothing happened for a few moments once we were inside, but then the cackling began. Anna shrieked and pointed above our heads where figures in cloaks leaped across the walls, looking down at us with glowing eyes before disappearing again. We turned into a shrouded clearing, where pale figures dressed like Civil War doctors loomed above a soldier who roared over the imminent loss of his limbs. Layla and Anna screamed and ran ahead. I grabbed Chloe's hand and pulled her through a break in the cornstalks, running wildly through a network of side paths left over from the farm's normal comings and goings.

"Uh-oh," I said. "We're lost."

"On purpose," Chloe said, picking a long blade of grass and chewing on it.

"What?" I said, tilting my voice up and stretching the word out for way too long. "I wouldn't do that."

"Right," Chloe said, looking at me stonily.

"Really though," I said after a moment of silence. "I actually have no idea where we are. Can you get us back to the path?"

"Just 'cause my parents own a farm," she said, crossing her arms, "you think I have, what, magic corn-vision?"

"Um...yes?" I said, biting my lip and shrugging.

She laughed once, softly, which made me feel a small sense of accomplishment.

She let out a long breath and looked up at the stars as we came to a branch in the path. "Just ask what you wanna ask."

"I don't know what you're talking about," I said, picking up a thin, bendy stick and swishing it hard across the leaves on the path. Chloe gave me a curious look. "In case we have to come back this way, we'll know where we've been before."

"Clever," Chloe said, nodding slowly.

"Thanks," I said, swishing the stick absent-mindedly. "So what's new in your world, Chloe?"

"Gotta turn around," she said, brushing past me as she doubled back. "Track curves away from where we need to be." We walked a bit further before she stopped and sighed, her shoulders slumping. "You really aren't gonna ask?" I shrugged and tried to appear as innocent as possible. "She dumped me."

"Oh," I said, long and soft. I took a few steps forward and wrapped her in a hug. "That sucks."

"I guess?" Chloe said, kneeling and ripping up a long, bendy stick of her own. We continued walking, me watching her as she swiped and slashed at the corn stalks. We only needed a few marks to find our way, but, I knew, sometimes people just needed to break things. "Yeah. It sucks."

"What happened?" We reached a fork that neither of

us had an immediate hunch about, so I flipped a coin and we went right. "You don't have to answer."

"No," Chloe said. "It's fine. Guess I'm not used to talking about it." She kicked a clump of dirt ahead of us and stared up at the stars. She was using more than five words at a time, which usually meant she was about to say something important. "You're only the second person who knows…about me."

"Bee was the first?" I said. She nodded. "That must have been lonely."

"Yeah," Chloe said. "We didn't have internet or anything on the farm when I was little. It was just me, my parents, my brothers, the animals and the farmhands. There was no place I could've learned about people like me. I thought I was the only one in the whole world when I was little."

"Jesus," I said, touching her shoulder.

"It was almost better," she said. "Before I knew how I was different it was just a vague notion. So much easier to ignore."

"But then Bee showed up?"

"Yep," Chloe said, sniffing sharply and tossing her stick aside. "Come on." She took my hand and pulled me through one of the corn walls. It was slow-going off the path, but I assumed she knew what she was doing.

"How long were y'all together?" I said as I tried to avoid tripping.

"'Bout a year," Chloe said.

"Wow," I said, thinking about how much I'd come to care for Grant in just the short time we'd been together. I paused for a moment, wanting to be careful with my next question. "Do you love her?"

"Thought so," Chloe said, pushing a cornstalk out of her way so hard it tipped over like a tree. "Till just now I thought so." She rubbed her hands on her jeans to clean the dirt off. "But what'd we really have in common?"

"Honestly?" I said as I sidled through the gap she'd made. "I'd have to say nothing."

"Right," Chloe said. "I just felt like she was my only option, and maybe in this town she is, but being alone's a perfectly good option for now." She stopped and turned to face me, her eyes glowing in the moonlight. "And I've got friends."

"You've got friends," I said, and this time she was the one who hugged me. "And hey," I said, as we pulled apart. "You're about to graduate. It's a big world." As I said the words, I couldn't help thinking about what I'd told Grant last night. But here in Lambertville, I realized, I didn't feel that same choking, desperate need to run away. For the first time ever I was living *my* life, the life I was supposed to live – I was finally the truest version of myself. I just happened to be keeping an enormous secret at the same time.

"You're right, I know. The world's waiting," Chloe said,

parting the final wall of corn to reveal the concessions area at the end of the maze.

"See," I said. "We found our way."

Chloe smiled wanly. "Somehow."

CHAPTER EIGHTEEN

I opened the door to find Grant standing in a black sweater, black jeans, and black sneakers, with mussed hair and his face painted to look like the cover of a Misfits album.

"Happy Halloween!" he said. His white teeth looked out of place in the middle of his messily painted face.

"No way," I said. He looked down at my bandolier, brown-and-tan tunic, leather trousers and knee-high boots and his eyes widened. "Is that really your costume?"

"Yeah?" he said, looking suddenly sheepish, which was strange coming from a face that could have belonged to the grim reaper. "This is what I do every year."

"Nope," I said, shaking my head. "Not this year. Come with me." I grabbed his hand and pulled him towards my bedroom.

"Hi, Mr Hardy," he said, waving and nearly stumbling over the coffee table.

"Happy Halloween, Grant," Dad said without looking up as he turned a page in the book he was reading. Grant had been coming to pick me up more lately and dropping by to say hi after work more often. Dad and I hadn't talked much since our fight that day in the Walmart parking lot, but we'd reached some sort of uneasy truce as we both went about our lives, getting ready for work and school, dinner in front of the TV.

"What are you supposed to be anyway?" Grant said as I plopped him on the bed and started digging through the box I'd had Mom ship to me a few weeks before.

"Remember in *Return of the Jedi*, when Leia disguises herself and comes to Jabba's palace to save Han?" I pointed to the helmet with the segmented mouthpiece and solid visor hanging off my bedpost, and Grant grinned like a little kid.

"Awesome," he said, only to widen his eyes when I showed him the Boba Fett helmet I'd just pulled out of the box. "What the hell? Where'd you get these?"

"Made them," I said absent-mindedly as I handed him the helmet and started pulling out the painted motorcycle jacket, trousers, boots and gloves that went with it.

"How'd you learn to make stuff like this?" he asked, holding the helmet out to inspect it, his voice reverent.

"I don't know," I said, tossing him the jacket and shrugging. I did know, of course: I had learned to make costumes the same year I learned to make sushi. "I used to have a lot more free time."

"Are you sure this stuff'll fit me?" Grant said, standing and holding the jacket against him. His face was already hidden behind the green-and-red helmet's opaque, T-shaped visor.

"It'll be tight," I said, "but yeah. We're almost the same height." I shrugged, embarrassed. "Sorry I'm such a giantess."

"I like it," he said, holding the helmet under his left arm and holding my hand with his right. "You're like... an Amazon."

"Nope," I said, poking him in the ribs with my elbow as I slipped my helmet on. "I'm not an Amazon. I'm a bounty hunter."

We made our way to the door, but Dad called for me just before I was out of earshot. Grant gave me a reassuring wave and jogged down the stairs while I stepped back inside.

"Yeah, Dad?"

"I've been thinking," he said, closing his book and sighing. "You're smart as a whip, and from everything I've heard from you and your mother you missed out on a lot of good years. It's okay if you want to cut loose a *little*. I haven't missed the fact that you're a teenager."

"Really?" I said, smiling despite myself.

"Do be careful though," he said, pointing his book at me.

170

"Of course," I said, nodding once, my heart lifting as I stepped towards the door. But before I left I turned around and met Dad's watery blue eyes. "And Dad? Thanks."

Our costumes were a sensation at Layla's Halloween party.

Half the people present weren't in costume at all, but Layla had had the forethought to put face paints out on the kitchen table next to the beer, and within an hour everyone who hadn't come with a costume had painted one on. Layla was dressed as Morticia Addams, skintight dress and all, and from the way she had to shuffle slowly to get anywhere I knew she had made the same style-over-function trade-off as Grant and me – our full-coverage helmets and leather jackets were a sweaty nightmare to dance in. Anna wasn't wearing a costume, because her parents would've killed her if they'd known she was coming to a Halloween party at all. Chloe's face was painted like a skull, and she was wearing black jeans and black boots. The only difference between her costume and Grant's original one was that she had on a flannel shirt instead of a black sweater.

"Aren't you glad?" I said, leaning on him as we rested in a corner and caught our breath. Our helmets sat on a side table next to us. He was on his fourth beer and I had just finished my second, feeling like a lightweight to already

171

be as giddy as I was. "Aren't you glad I spared you the embarrassment? Nothing worse than showing up to a party in the same outfit as another girl."

"Is that a thing?" he said.

"Oh yeah," I said. "Stuff like that can be a *total* social disaster."

"Being a girl seems like it has a lotta rules," he said, sounding suddenly thoughtful.

"Oh totally," I said, thinking of the million things I had to learn to fit in. "It's way harder than being a guy."

"What?" Grant said. "No way. When's the last time you got in a fist-fight? You ever been popped in the nose?"

I remembered all the times guys had hit and kicked me because they didn't like me, but decided it was best not to mention those. "Whatever, tough guy." I poked him in the chest and put a hand on my hip. "A fist-fight gets you a black eye but girls *destroy* each other with just a couple of words. Guys could never handle what we go through."

"Challenge accepted!" Grant said, setting his beer down and grabbing his helmet. "Come with me." He grabbed my wrist and dragged me in to Layla's hall bathroom, slamming the door shut behind us.

"What're you doing?" I said, confused.

"You called me out," he said as he unzipped the Boba Fett jacket and tossed it to my side of the bathroom. "Now we gotta switch costumes."

"What?" I said, the room tilting ever so slightly. I leaned against the sink for balance. He was down to a tank top, boxers and socks. "Why?"

"You said I ain't got the guts to be a girl," he said, "and I don't back down from a challenge. Gimme your costume."

I stripped down to a cami and boyshorts, giggling the whole time, and watched as he clumsily got into the bounty-hunter Leia costume. Once everything was zipped up and the helmet was on I had to admit that besides the broader shoulders and a certain flatness across the chest, nobody would know the difference – provided he kept the helmet on, of course.

"What am I supposed to wear?" I said.

"You get to be Boba Fett," he said. "Let's see if you got the *guts* to be a boy."

I looked down at the Boba Fett mask, then at myself in the mirror, and started laughing. I doubled over, wrapping my arms around myself and nearly falling over.

"What's so funny?" Grant said.

"Nothing," I gasped, slowly getting myself back under control. I wiped away a tear and started getting dressed, shaking my head. There was something hilarious about the idea of me dressing as a boy, after so many years of trying to escape it. "Nothing. You go on. I'll come out once I'm dressed."

I stepped out of the bathroom a few minutes later to find the party even more raucous than we had left it.

The beer was almost completely finished, and the way the partygoers leaned on one another and howled out of key to "Monster Mash" and "Thriller" told me exactly where it had gone. I stood there awkwardly for a moment, unsure what to do. Wearing boys' clothes, even a costume, felt like a skin I'd long ago shed.

"Grant!" somebody called from over near the kitchen. I looked around for Grant, and then the voice called out again and I realized they were calling to me. Two guys I recognized from the football team were standing in a cluster near the stove, beckoning me. Parker stood just behind them, a beer in his hand, trying to look nonchalant. I walked over to them, only to realize a few steps in that my wrists were too loose, my elbows tucked in at my sides, my hips swaying slightly. That wasn't how boys walked. I pushed my elbows and knees out and tried to keep my spine as stiff as possible. When I reached the kitchen Grant's friends looked confused.

"You okay?" one of the guys said. He had whiskers and a cat nose painted on his face.

"Yeah," I said, deepening my voice. I was glad to hear the helmet muffled my words.

"You were walking like you shit your pants," Kitten Face said, wearing a look of genuine concern.

"I know what it is," the other guy said. He had fake stitching painted from the corners of his mouth up to his cheekbones so he looked like a rag doll. He leaned

174

over and punched me hard in the arm. I tried not to make a sound. "I saw you go in the bathroom with that chick."

"She's so hot, dude," rag-doll guy said. "What'd you guys do in there?"

"Yeah," Kitten Face said, leaning close. "She finally put out?" I saw Parker trying to pretend he wasn't watching us. He snorted and rolled his eyes.

When I didn't answer, Rag Doll leaned close. "She at least let you see her tits?"

I punched him in the arm harder than I meant to and headed back towards the keg. "I'm gonna grab another beer."

"What crawled up his ass?" I heard Kitten Face say behind me as I walked away from them and through the crush of bodies in the living room.

Outside, I got in Dad's car and turned the radio to the classical station that just barely came in. With the helmet off and the window rolled down I could breathe again. My stomach felt like it was on a gyroscope, spinning and twirling. I pressed my forehead to the steering wheel and groaned, trying to centre myself. I knew how guys talked about girls when they weren't around, of course. I shouldn't have been surprised. But those two reminded me of the guys who tormented me when I was younger, and it still struck a nerve with me, no matter how much had changed. A knock at the window made me jump.

"Give up already?" Grant said. His hair was plastered to his scalp. He panted as he sat in the passenger seat.

"Yeah," I said, turning just enough that I could keep my forehead on the cool steering wheel while also making eye contact with him. "Your friends are creeps, by the way."

"What friends?" Grant said.

"The guy with the cat paint and the one with the rag-doll paint."

He thought about that for a moment. "Oh, those guys are assholes. They're not my friends, they're just on the team."

"Good," I said, squeezing his hand and smiling. "How did you do?"

"I'm not sure," Grant said. "Chloe hugged me and thanked me for 'that corn thing the other day'." I laughed. "And, uh, I kind of…" He mumbled something I couldn't make out.

"What was that?" I said.

"I got flirted with a bunch!" he said, his cheeks glowing bright pink.

"By guys?" I said, sitting up straight.

"They thought I was you!" he said, crossing his arms.

"Did you flirt back?" I said, leaning forward and grinning.

"No!" he said. "Jesus."

"You liked it!" I said. He rolled his eyes but the pink on his cheeks didn't go away. "Come on, admit you had fun.

It's okay. The whole point of Halloween is pretending."

"Yeah," he said, looking thoughtful. "It's weird to be someone else for a little while."

"Yeah," I said, shifting closer to him and resting my head on his chest. The bass, still audible out here, formed a steady rhythm, with the happy shrieks of partiers rising above the din.

"You know when I was a kid, the first time I watched *Star Wars*, it was like, I don't know, like my whole world opening up," Grant said suddenly. I left my head where it was, enjoying the rise and fall of his chest. "It sounds stupid now, but seeing those characters with their crazy outfits, those badass spaceships, I started to think that maybe there was more out there than football and playin' in dirt."

I nodded, thinking of the first time I had watched the movie too. I had loved to escape into science fiction and fantasy for as long as I could remember, loved anything where the main characters didn't look like the people I saw around me, and especially anything with themes of acceptance and social injustice. But my relationship with sci-fi was a little more complicated than Grant's, because it was one of the things about me that was typically male. I knew that some girls had grown up reading comic books, but since my transition, I wasn't sure whether it was something I should hide, like my encyclopedic knowledge of every episode of *Deep Space Nine* might somehow out me.

I loved that I didn't have to hide it from Grant.

"I don't know what I'm really tryin' to say," Grant continued. "It helps to think about things other'n yourself, imagine that there's a different way to be, I guess."

I sat up and kissed him long and hard, to tell him everything I couldn't articulate – that for a guy who'd rarely received better than a C in school, for someone who thought the most value he brought was knocking guys over on a football field, he was one of the smartest people I had ever met.

I lay back down against him and we listened to the party go on without us, our breaths syncing. As I felt Grant's heart beat in his chest, a thought that both thrilled and terrified me snaked its way from my stomach to the tips of my fingers: I was falling in love with him.

CHAPTER NINETEEN

"Sorry for skipping out on you last week," I said, tying my hair up against the wind as I mounted the warped old plantation steps. Bee glanced up at me before returning her gaze to her camera's viewfinder.

"S'fine," she said, scooting over to make room for me on the step. I brushed the papery leaves away and sat down. "I know how it goes."

"Yeah. How are you holding up, by the way?" I said as I dropped my backpack between my knees and pulled out my chemistry homework.

"Fine," Bee said, giving me a strange look when she finally noticed the note of concern in my voice. "Why?"

"Well, you and Chloe were a pretty big deal, weren't you?"

"I don't know," Bee said, twisting a knob and pointing the lens out at the horizon. "Hey, I don't have any portraits in my portfolio yet." She lowered the camera again and looked at me. "Mind if I take your picture?"

"I guess not," I said, tapping a pencil against my notepad and looking down at the grass. "Chloe seemed to think y'all were pretty serious."

"Yeah," Bee said, scratching her temple. "That was the problem. She thought things were more serious than I did. If she were a guy I'd have bailed as soon as I realized she wanted more from me than sex and the occasional hangout."

"How did her being a girl make it different?"

Bee looked up from her work to stare into the middle distance. "The first time we ever kissed she cried in my arms, because she'd spent her whole life trying to pretend those feelings weren't real. She told me she couldn't decide if she was disgusted with herself or proud that she'd finally had the strength to do what she wanted. She said she thought she was the only one."

"That's so sad," I said, trying to imagine Chloe crying.

"But obviously that just isn't true," Bee went on. She pulled out her phone and looked at it for a moment before continuing. "So there's about seven thousand, four hundred people in Lambertville, and queer people represent about ten per cent of the population. That's, what, seven hundred and forty people right there. Let's assume women are an even half of that, and you can assume there are three hundred and ninety bisexual or lesbian women in this town."

"That seems high," I said, though I couldn't help wondering whether any other people like me lived here in secret as well.

"It seems high because queer people in the South are addicted to the closet," she said, furrowing her brow and digging in her camera bag for a different lens. "Hell, even the straight people have enough skeletons in their closet to fill a tomb. Everybody's too afraid of going to hell or getting made fun of to be honest about what they want and who they are, so they can't even really admit what they want to themselves. It's sad."

"Yeah." I was nodding, but I wondered what Bee would say if I told her the truth – that I was one of those people who wasn't being honest. It struck me, in a way it hadn't before, that Bee was pretty brave, just for being herself.

"But anyway, I realized I was with her out of obligation, and that is absolutely not something I do, so I broke up with her."

"But you must've realized that a while ago…you were together a long time, right? So why now?" I folded and unfolded a page in my textbook absent-mindedly. "Was there somebody else?"

"Different subject?" Bee said, looking exhausted. "I know I hurt her, but she was gonna get hurt one way or the other. Just drop it, okay?"

"Sure," I said, biting my thumbnail. "Sorry."

"Make it up to me by sitting up straight and looking at that weird-looking tree," she said, pointing across the clearing.

"That's a Bradford pear," I said, squaring my shoulders. The camera stayed silent. "They're bred to have this beautiful vertical branch pattern, but trees aren't supposed to grow that way, which is why they look the way they do. They grow fast though, so real estate agents like to plant them to sell properties quick and then the trunks don't start twisting up and dying like that until a few years after."

"Where the hell'd you learn that?" Bee said as the camera clicked away.

"My mom's a real estate agent."

Bee smiled. "All right," she said. "At first you looked like a robot, but I got some good shots there at the end."

"I look like a robot?" I said, frowning.

"Not you, just that face. Try smiling." I smiled. "Okay, wow, you look like somebody's got a gun on you just outside the frame. You're one of those people."

"What people?"

"*Earnest* people," she said, as if that should mean something to me. "You're just so repulsively honest that you can't even fake feelings when you want to."

"I don't think that's true," I said, thinking of my relationship with Grant, how sometimes it felt like I was telling him everything about me except the single biggest thing.

"Whatever," Bee said. "I know how to deal with people like you." She adjusted the lens and pointed it at me again. "The only way to fight earnestness is with earnestness. Remember back when we'd just met, and we played the honesty game?"

"Yeah," I said, my mouth feeling suddenly dry.

"Well, my biggest secret isn't that I'm bi," Bee said, leaning forward slightly. I cocked my head and listened. "I was raped in tenth grade."

"Oh my God," I said, covering my mouth and leaning forward. "I'm so sorry."

"Whatever," Bee said, waving my condolences away and snapping a few pictures. "It's not a…I mean, it was a big deal. I needed therapy and shit. But it's not why I am who I am or whatever. Anyway, that's not the secret." She took a few steps backwards and kneeled, the camera still pointed at me. "The secret's coming."

I nodded and looked away from her, off into the distance, where the wind rustled the grass like a gentle wave. By not looking at her, it felt like I was giving Bee privacy to tell her secret, somehow.

"So the guy who did it was a senior at one of the private schools up in Knoxville. His dad owns like seventy-five per cent of this shitsburg, which is, I guess, why he was down here at the time. My folks told me I needed to go to the police. They got real mad at me because I was hesitating about it. But, like…everybody'd been calling me a slut since sixth grade when I had the bad luck to grow boobs first, and it felt like the son of a bitch's family had enough money that there was no point, and really I just wanted the whole thing behind me, so I went to therapy and got over it and moved on."

"And then?" I said, wanting to cross the distance between us and hug her. But something told me she needed to keep going, so I stayed where I was.

"And then two years later he was arrested anyway," Bee said, her voice brittle and distant. "He'd got four more girls after me. One was twelve." She lowered the camera for a moment and rubbed her eyes. "And it's like, the rape was something I could put behind me, at least most days. I don't really think about it, any more. But if I'd come forward, yeah, he might not've gone to jail, but it would've been in the news, and those girls and their parents would've had a chance of avoiding what happened. That's harder to get over." She bit her lip and slowly started bringing the camera back up. "Therapy hasn't really helped with *that*."

"Bee," I said softly.

The camera clicked a half-dozen times. Her hands shook. I wanted to comfort her, but there was nothing I could say. Everything that came to mind sounded empty. I wanted to give her something real, to show her that she

184

was right to trust me, that I trusted her too. Only one thing came to mind.

"I was close to telling you something last time we played," I said, keeping my voice low.

"Sure," Bee said, still sounding a little shaken.

"It's serious though," I said, raising my eyebrows. The camera clicked over and over. "Really. I'm not kidding. It's not about me being embarrassed, or worried what people will think. It's much bigger than that." She looked up from the viewfinder and blinked. "If you tell people what I'm about to tell you, it will end me."

"I won't tell," Bee said quietly. The look on her face was the most serious I had ever seen her wear.

"You promise?"

"I promise."

"Okay," I said, scooting back to my side and looking out at the grass shivering in the wind as it gave in to the inevitability of winter. I breathed cool air in through my nose, held it, and poured it back out between my teeth. Now was my chance to stop. But I didn't. "I'm transsexual."

For a moment, Bee didn't say anything. Then she spoke. "Do I have your permission to take a few more photos?" she asked. "I have some questions, but the way you look right now is really important to me and I want to keep it." I nodded. The camera clicked faster than ever and then suddenly stopped. I felt a wave of naked warmth climb up my neck and down from my shoulders as she

185

lowered the camera and stared at me. "I've never met anybody like you," she said.

"Most people haven't," I said. I was surprised my voice wasn't shakier. I looked down at my hands and saw they were relatively still. "Or at least they don't know they have."

"Okay," Bee said, nodding slowly. "I've seen...what's the word? Transgendered?"

"'Trans people' is best," I said, my voice barely above a whisper.

"I've seen trans people in movies and TV shows, but judging by how unrealistic and shitty bi characters tend to be, I'm gonna assume I know nothing. So what's okay for me to ask?"

"Don't ask about my genitals," I said, balling up my skirt and looking up at the clouds. "Just don't."

"Wouldn't matter," Bee said, shrugging.

"Thanks." I bit my lip. "Don't ask about surgeries. Don't ask what my name used to be. That's pretty much it."

"Okay," Bee said. She put her camera away, folding the strap deliberately, her eyes locked on something just beneath the deck. "You didn't have to tell me," she said.

"I wanted to," I said, releasing my skirt and surprising myself with a smile. "I really wanted to."

"Well, you should know I was just fucking with you earlier," Bee said, "with the stuff about the robot." She rubbed the back of her neck and I was almost sure I saw her cheeks redden before she turned to pick up something behind her.

"I figured," I said, my smile widening. Seeing Bee vulnerable was almost as weird as seeing emotion from my dad.

"But you know you're gorgeous, right?" she said, shouldering her bag and turning back around. If there had been a blush it was gone. I put my homework away and stood with her.

"Thanks. You know what happened to those girls wasn't your fault, right?" I said. I crossed the distance like I'd wanted to before and swept her into a hug. We stood like that, our arms around each other for a long while, longer, maybe, than I'd ever hugged anyone before. "Bee, I'm really glad I met you."

"I'm glad I met you too."

OCTOBER, SIX YEARS AGO

Marcus didn't save me a seat on the bus the first Monday after our sleepover.

We didn't always sit together but I didn't mind; he was really cute and smart, and he had a lot of friends, so he tried to spend time with as many of them as he could. That was why our friendship meant so much to me, really – he could have spent time with anybody, and he wanted to spend time with me. His friendship had been one of the best parts of seventh grade, maybe the only good part. But as I stared at the back of Marcus's head, I could tell something was off. He hadn't even made eye contact with me in math, and when I'd tried to flag him down after class ended and ask if he wanted to hang out again next weekend, he'd looked away from me and walked faster.

As the rolling hills outside the bus windows turned into perfectly manicured lawns, I stared straight ahead and tried to imagine what I could have done to upset him. He got off at the same stop as me; I would try to talk to him again when we were alone.

I was already on my feet when the bus hissed to a stop. Marcus stopped when his feet hit the sidewalk and stared at me while the bus churned back to life and rumbled away.

"Hey," I said, wondering why he was looking at me like that. "How was your day?"

"I don't want to talk to you," Marcus said, scowling and turning his face away. He put a hand on his backpack strap and turned to walk away.

"Did I do something wrong?" I said, hating how wimpy and desperate I sounded. But I needed to know.

Marcus dropped his backpack onto the ground and pulled a bent black composition book out.

"That's my diary," I said, as a wave of sheer horror shot through me.

"Boys call them journals, faggot," he said in a low, dangerous voice. He started reading from the open page. "'So glad I haven't hit puberty yet. Maybe I'll be lucky and I never will, or maybe everybody is wrong and when I go through puberty I will turn into a woman like I'm supposed to. Probably not, but at least I can dream'."

"Stop," I said, looking around to make sure the street was clear. "Please stop."

"'Marcus is so gorgeous,'" he read, his voice lowering.

189

He glanced up at me, his brows knitted. "*'I wish we could do more on our sleepovers, but just being near him is nice'.*" He turned a page. I ran over and tried to grab the journal out of his hands. He struggled with me for a moment and then punched me in the stomach. I gagged wordlessly and fell to my knees, my hands over my aching gut. "*'Maybe one day I can finally be a girl like I'm supposed to, and then he'll see how I feel about him, and maybe he'll feel the same way.'*" He turned the page again. I didn't stand back up but felt tears dripping out of my closed eyes.

"*'It isn't because he's so hot though, really,'*" Marcus continued. "*'It's because of how wonderful he is.'*" His voice faltered at the end. "I never read this part." He was silent for a moment, then continued. "*'He's smart, and funny, and never cruel'.*" Marcus's voice was lower now, almost a whisper. "*'Nobody has ever been as nice to me as he is. He's made me feel like maybe the world isn't so bad, since he's in it.'*"

"Oh God," I said, rocking gently. "Sorry, sorry. I'm so sorry."

"What are you?" he said, stepping back. I couldn't look up at him. I stared at the cracks in the sidewalk and slowly shook my head.

"I don't know," I said. "I don't know."

"Well, whatever you are, never come near me again," he said as he threw my diary on the ground between us and walked away.

CHAPTER
TWENTY

Virginia was late.

I sat at the bar in the Sartoris Diner and read *Absalom, Absalom!* for class, trying to figure out which character disgusted me the most. The waitress refilled my Diet Coke and I checked my texts for the dozenth time since Virginia had contacted me an hour before, saying she was going to be near Lambertville and that she wanted to see me.

Where are you? I typed.

Pulling in now, she responded. *Sorry, GPS isn't much use in the boonies.*

I turned and saw her banged-up Bronco pulling up. The door chimed as she came in. I ran over and wrapped my arms around her before it had time to close.

"Easy, girl!" she said, laughing and half-heartedly

trying to push me away. "Jesus, how starved for company are you?"

"It's not that," I said, retreating a step and bouncing on my toes. "I just missed *you*!"

"Same, kid," she said, giving me a crooked smile as we settled in at the bar. "We've all been worried sick about you."

"How is everybody?" I asked. The waitress came by. I ordered a waffle and Virginia ordered a plate of hash browns.

"Same old bullshit," Virginia said, rolling her eyes as she took a sip of water, "or so I hear. I've been in Knoxville almost as long as you've been here."

"Why?"

"Tinder hook-up at first," she said. I looked away and she laughed. "Still a prude! Anyway, it turned out he was one of the, like, five guys on the planet who's willing to date trans women without being a creep about it." My heart raced suddenly and I glanced at the waitress and cook to see if they'd heard her. The cook was scraping gunk off the grill and the waitress was cutting up lemons. "What's up?" Virginia said, giving me a small wave.

"Nothing," I said, turning my attention to my waffle even though my appetite had disappeared.

"I've known your neurotic ass long enough to know when something's up," she said.

"It's just," I began, then halted and took a deep breath.

I felt like the worst friend ever, but she had insisted. "It's just that I'm trying to be stealth."

"Ah," Virginia said. She squirted hot sauce on her hash browns and shrugged, though her expression was hard to read. "I get it. I won't use the *T* word again."

"Okay," I said, forcing myself to smile. "Thanks."

"Don't mention it," she said. "So anyway, he was cool but things didn't work out."

"Why not?" I said, straightening my back and facing her again.

"He said he could deal with me being...the way I am, but that he wanted a family one day and, since I couldn't provide that, it felt like we were going nowhere."

"Ouch," I said, my stomach churning as I imagined a grown-up Grant saying the same thing to me.

"Whatever," Virginia said. "It is what it is. How are things with your guy?"

"Good," I said, rubbing my arm. "We kind of had our first fight, but we got over it, and things have been great ever since."

"Aww," she said.

I looked up at her and took a deep breath. "Do you think I should tell him?"

"Hell no!" she said, arching an eyebrow and leaning away from me. "Why would you do that?"

"I don't know," I said, scrunching my nose and sighing. "I feel like maybe he should know who I am..."

"You don't owe it to him if *that's* what you're thinking," she said. "You're a girl, you've always been a girl, you won the genetic lottery when it comes to passing, and he'll never ever have to know unless he sees your birth certificate for some reason."

"Or wants to get married or start a family," I said, jabbing my straw at the ice clattering in my now-empty cup. "But that's not why."

"First of all, you're only eighteen," Virginia said, her cheek full of fried potatoes. She poked her fork at me for emphasis. "You're supposed to be having *real* fun for the first time in your life, not dreaming of settling down with Mr Right."

"Whatever!" I said, flipping my hair and sticking my tongue out at her. "I like him a lot...I think I might love him." I chose to ignore Virginia rolling her eyes. "And it obviously isn't everything, but being...being *the way I am* has been a huge part of my life. It's easy to act like my past never happened, but it feels like I've put up this wall around my heart."

"You know walls are there for a reason though, right?" she said as she gingerly wiped hot sauce off her fingers. "They keep things from falling apart." I started to say something but she held up a hand. "That's just my opinion. Do what you want with it."

"That's fair," I said. I made a motion to the waitress that we were ready for the bill. "How long are you in town?"

"However long I feel like, I guess," Virginia said, shrugging with one shoulder as she rummaged for her wallet. "So what's up for tonight? Should we call your friends?"

"Oh," I said, my hand freezing between my phone and my face. I looked Virginia up and down and saw two separate people. One was the beautiful, statuesque angel who had been there to guide me through some of the hardest steps of my transition. The other was a woman with a jaw just a little too strong, forehead just a little too high, shoulders just a little too wide, and hands just a little too big. I felt like an ungrateful bitch for thinking like that at all, but a hateful little voice at the back of my head screamed that if my friends saw me with her, and if my friends figured out *she* was trans, then they might figure me out next.

"What?" Virginia said. She looked over her shoulder and then looked at me, her shoulders tightening as she bit her fingernail. Then, as I sat mute, her expression began to darken. "Oh," she said finally. "Oh, I get it. Amanda, hey, don't look so stricken. It's okay if you don't want me to meet your friends. You don't have to worry about my feelings."

"No!" I said, shaking my head and blinking. "I mean, yes. It's complicated, but…" I trailed off, pain and confusion mingling in my chest. Virginia had meant so much to me for so long, and I wanted her to meet all the people who were beginning to mean a lot to me now.

A sudden thought occurred to me, and I slid my phone out from my pocket. "There is one person, actually," I told her with a smile.

"So what do people do for fun around here?" Virginia asked as we pulled out of Bee's driveway.

"Meth, mostly," Bee said from the back seat. I craned my neck and saw her fishing for something in her bag. "Mind if I smoke?"

"I don't know," Virginia said. She reached up and poked at one of the torn, hanging strips of upholstery above her. "I'd hate it if the smell messed up my car's trade-in value."

Bee's sudden laughter catapulted her unlit cigarette into the front seat.

"I like her!" Bee said, leaning forward to grab her cigarette where it had landed in a cup holder. "What was your name again?"

"Virginia," she said.

"And how do you guys know each other?"

"Virginia's my trans mentor," I replied.

Virginia raised an eyebrow. "What happened to being stealth?"

"She's the only one I told," I explained.

Virginia looked in the rear-view mirror for a long

time, then to the road, then back at me. She seemed to be evaluating something, but she didn't say anything more.

"So where are you girls taking me?" Bee said as she ashed her cigarette out the window.

Virginia didn't hesitate. "A gay bar in Chattanooga called Mirages," she said, grinning in the rear-view.

"Hell yeah!" Bee cried, slapping the back of the seat. "Are all your trans friends as badass as her?"

"Nope!" I said happily. "Virginia's one in a million."

As the interstate flew by outside the car, Virginia asking all the right questions and making Bee laugh, I smiled. She really was one in a million – she was the sister I never had, the watchful eye that had kept me safe, and I hated myself for ever thinking her anything but beautiful. I thought about how every person could hold two truths inside of them, how impossible it felt sometimes to have your insides and outsides aligned.

The conversation flowed as Bee and Virginia moved on to college plans, previous relationships, and tales of debauchery.

"I'm glad you guys like each other," I said after a while, smiling. It had taken me a little while to figure out what I was feeling, but now I understood: it was the sense of two parts of me coming together. It felt honest.

"Sorry I'm being quiet," I said. "I'm just…happy. This isn't something I felt like I could ever have."

Virginia smiled at me in the rear-view, warm and wise. "You can have anything," she said, "once you admit you deserve it."

CHAPTER
TWENTY-ONE

I sat on the balcony with my laptop and a glass of sweet tea, enjoying the crisp fall weather and nursing what remained of a hangover while I tried – and failed – to finish a paper on *Absalom*. We'd got in late last night, and Virginia had left early this morning, before Dad even woke up. Part of me wanted them to meet, but another part of me was glad they hadn't. The night with Bee had been great, but not everyone was Bee.

I sipped my tea and stared at the blank Word document on my laptop's screen. The sun was setting, casting an orange glow over the parking lot below and the woods beyond. I thought of the cicadas, long gone by now, and listened to the rustling, howling wind that had taken their place. Grant's shift at McDonald's would be ending in a little over an hour. The thought that had been bubbling just under the surface for weeks arose once more, unbidden:

What if I told Grant the truth?

"I can't do it," I said to nobody in particular. I'd been able to tell Bee because I'd got swept up in the moment, and because I knew that even if she didn't understand, she'd try to. But what about Grant? Was it crazy that I wanted to tell him everything? Was it crazy that I felt like I couldn't keep seeing him without at least trying?

I sat up straight again, took a deep breath, and opened my eyes to see the blank Word document still waiting for me. The cursor blinked over and over, like a promise, or a threat.

Dear Grant, I wrote after a moment. *This is the story of my life. When I was born my parents named me Andrew Hardy and the doctors wrote "male" on my birth certificate. They had no idea who I would grow up to be.*

I stood in the employee parking lot behind McDonald's, my stomach in a knot. I had already been waiting for an hour, but it felt like ten hours and like five minutes all at once. The envelope in my hands was thick and crumpled at the corners from my constant fidgeting.

Inside it was a letter that told him everything: my birth name, my suicide attempt, how long I had been on hormones, the effects hormones had had, and the bathroom assault that pushed me into his life. Everything.

The back door opened, casting a rectangle of light across the pavement. I clutched the envelope tighter.

"Night, Greg," Grant said, and I could see the sweat stains on his back. I thought of how he'd looked that first night with his shirt off, and of how he always smelled when he got sweaty, like dirt and salt and things I couldn't name.

"Hi," I said. He took in one sharp breath and stopped, his eyes glinting in the reflected light of a passing car. I opened Dad's car door so the interior light revealed me and waved. I crossed into the darkness to meet him, feeling gangly and awkward, and gently pressed the envelope to his chest.

"You've shared some things with me, and now, I want to share some things with you," I told him softly.

"Thank you," Grant said. I saw the outline of his head lean down and then back up. "What is this?"

"It's everything," I said, my mouth and throat dry. We were both silent for a moment. "Just, ahead of time, I wanted to let you know – if you're upset with me for letting things progress like they did, for being with you…I'm sorry for that too, and I understand."

He stood there for a long time, unreadable in the darkness. My heart started racing again and my stomach flipped back and forth, so I focused on the pavement beneath us, tracing its infinite cracks. When I looked up again Grant was gone. My heart hammered for one horrible moment before he came back outside, carrying the unopened envelope and a metal bucket.

The small flame of a butane lighter flickered to life. The orange glow flared brightly as Grant held the lighter to the envelope and it caught fire. I gasped and started to ask what he was doing, but he dropped the envelope into the bucket, where its warmth and light bathed both of us. I felt myself starting to cry until I looked at his face and noticed he was smiling.

"I'll never regret being with you," he said, reaching out for my hand. "And I could never, ever hate you, no matter what."

"But—" I said.

"I never needed to know," he said, shaking his head. "I just needed to feel like you'd given me a chance."

He pulled me around the fire, wrapped me in the tightest embrace I could remember, and kissed me like the fire burning brightly beside us.

SIX MONTHS AGO

I took a dose of hydrocodone when I was done dilating. Everything between my thighs and my hips felt like it had been run through a wood chipper, the dilation ritual was a degrading chore, the painkillers reminded me of the time I tried to kill myself – and I still couldn't have been happier. I was finally a girl on the outside too; there was nothing separating me from my body any more. As the painkillers kicked in I swung my feet off the bed, winced, and shuffled slowly into the hall. I stopped halfway to the bathroom when I heard the soft sound of crying further along. I made my way to the den and found Mom huddled up on the floor beside a single dim lamp, photo albums spread open around her.

"Mom?" I said. She jumped and cried out, then put a hand over her heart and closed her eyes when she realized it was me. "What's going on?"

"Nothing," she said, shaking her head and wiping her nose. "Just reorganizing our photos before I go to bed. Now scoot, you need your rest."

"No," I said. I winced again as I slowly kneeled down. She looked like she wanted to snap all the albums closed, but she left them where they were. One was open to pictures of me, Mom and Dad at the beach when I was three or four. I was running happily through flocks of seagulls, squealing in delight as I ran away from waves that seemed so large at the time. Another was open to me in preschool, with my shaggy little ringlets and my smile missing its teeth. The rest were open to my pages as well: a photo of me winning a spelling bee; graduating from elementary school; looking distracted at Rock City and Ruby Falls in Chattanooga the day we left Dad, up to the last pictures where I still looked like a boy.

"I miss him," Mom whispered, her eyes cast to the side.

"Dad?" I said.

"No," Mom said, and I heard her throat clenching. A tear streaked down her cheek, but it wasn't followed by any others. "No, I miss my son."

"Oh!" I said, dropping the album page I was holding. "Oh."

"I'm sorry," Mom said, shaking her head and swallowing. "I'm sorry, really. I thought you were asleep."

"I'm still me," I said, trying to catch her eye again.

"It ain't that simple," Mom said, opening her watery

eyes and returning them to me. "I know I'm supposed to say it is, but it ain't. You look different, you act different, you sound different, your hands feel different when I touch 'em. Hell, you even *smell* different. Do you know how important smell can be, how the way your baby smells when you hold him gets locked in your head?"

I clenched my fingers. "Why didn't you tell me?"

"You tried to kill yourself," she said, rolling her eyes up to heaven and biting her knuckle. "Andrew Hardy was gonna die one way or the other, and one of the choices gave me a daughter in exchange while the other left me with no one."

"I never thought of it that way," I said. "I never thought about—"

"It ain't your responsibility to comfort your parents," she said, shaking her head. " 'Least, not until I start needin' *my* diapers changed." She started closing the albums again. "And anyway this ain't the first time I mourned my baby." She took a shuddering breath.

"What do you mean?" I tried to help her stack the albums back up and put them away, but she slapped my hands and quickly did it herself.

"No strenuous activity!" she said, and then she lowered herself into an overstuffed chair by the bookshelf and closed her eyes again. "When you were a year old I looked at your baby pictures and cried. When you were three I looked at the pictures from when you were one and cried.

When you went to kindergarten I looked back and cried. Kids constantly grow and change, and every time you blink they turn into something different and the kid you thought you had is just a memory." She rubbed her sinuses and sighed. "Five years from now you'll be a grown woman graduatin' college and I'll look at photos of you now and grieve my teenage daughter."

"So I shouldn't feel guilty?"

"'Course you should!" she said with a broad smile. "You got any idea what you've done to me? Between the labour pain and the stretch marks and the loans I had to take out for this surgery, you've bled me dry!"

"I'll make it up to you one day," I said resolutely as I braced myself against the bookshelf and stood again.

"When you're rich and famous?" Mom said, smiling now.

"Yup," I said as I turned and headed back to the bathroom. I looked over my shoulder as I entered the hallway. "Rich, anyway. Famous is for chumps." I got to the bathroom and yelled, "I love you, by the way!"

"Are you in the bathroom?" she called in response. I didn't answer, but Mom quickly said, "Gross, Amanda," anyway.

CHAPTER
TWENTY-TWO

"**W**here are Layla and Anna?" I asked as I took my seat at our regular lunch table. I was lucky enough to have the same lunch period as all three girls on most days, and they always saved me a seat. For the first time in my life I actually looked forward to walking into the cafeteria.

"Homecoming committee," Chloe replied through a mouthful of tater tots. She swallowed and gave me a bashful look. "Sorry. Manners."

"It's cool," I said, pulling out my Tupperware. "I mean you *were* raised in a barn."

"Whatever!" she said, lobbing a tater tot at me. It bounced off my collarbone before tumbling into the front of my shirt. "Deserved it," she said. I fished the tater tot out of my bra and laughed.

Chloe rolled her rectangular piece of cafeteria pizza up

and took a bite as if it were a burrito. This time she waited until after swallowing to talk. "Grant asked you to homecoming yet?"

"No!" I said, stabbing at my salad. The posters had been up at school for weeks now, and every time I passed one, I felt tiny pinpricks all over my skin. Grant cared about me, I knew he did, so I didn't understand why he hadn't asked me. All my old fears were stirring just below the surface, threatening to rise. "I'm starting to think he doesn't want to go with me."

"Better man up soon," Chloe said, but there was a strange pitch to her voice.

I started to respond, but then she shot up and called out, "Here she is!" I turned just in time to see six guys in football pads and black-and-white paper Stormtrooper masks rushing towards me. Years of bullying made me panic as they lifted me from the ground.

"Easy," one of the guys whispered. I recognized Grant's friend Rodney's voice. "Easy. We ain't gonna hurt you."

Chloe swept into view with her camera held out, recording. I forced myself to relax – she was clearly in on whatever was happening. The guys hoisted me onto their shoulders and hustled me out of the cafeteria to a din of confused laughter.

My captors kicked in the double doors to the gymnasium to reveal Grant in a white long-sleeve shirt and black trousers with white stripes up the side. On one side of him stood a guy in a paper Darth Vader mask with a cheap-looking black cape, and on the other, someone wore the Boba Fett costume I had given to Grant after Halloween.

"Leia!" Grant said. He rushed forward, pretending to be restrained when Vader and Fett grabbed his arms.

"Han!" I said, laughing as the football-players-turned-Stormtroopers set me down before him.

"What if he dies?" Boba Fett said, his voice raspy and his delivery stiff.

"The Empire will compensate you if he dies," a goofily deep voice said. I thought I recognized it as Parker's, but I wasn't sure. "Any last words, Solo?"

"Leia!" Grant said, really hamming it up in his attempt to break free. "Will you come to homecoming with me?"

"Of course!" I cried, stepping forward and clasping my hands over my heart. I started to say "I love you!" since that was the next line, but paused. We hadn't said those words yet, although I couldn't help thinking it all the time lately. Instead I declared, "I...like you! A lot!"

"I know," Grant said, donning a perfect Han Solo smirk all the same. I wondered what was going to come next, since a carbonite freezing chamber seemed out of the question, and then the Stormtroopers pulled out aerosol cans, shook them, and sprayed both of us with Silly String.

* * *

Darth Vader was waiting for me outside the bathroom when I finally got the silly string off my hands and face.

"Lord Vader," I said. "I should have known. Only you could be so bold."

"Uh," Vader said. He pulled the mask down to reveal Parker's confused face. "I don't know the next line. Sorry."

"It's fine," I said, forcing a smile. Parker was often at parties with us, or on the outskirts of smaller groups, but hadn't said much to me since my early days in Lambertville. "Thanks for helping with that whole...thing."

"Promposal?" Parker said, scrunching up one side of his face. "I think that's what we're calling it now."

"'Homecomingposal' doesn't really roll off the tongue," I noted. He chuckled and shook his head.

"That it don't," he said. He frowned at his feet and rubbed the back of his neck, then made eye contact with me again with what looked like effort. "I've been meanin' to tell you I'm sorry."

"What for?"

"Bein' a dick at that party, like a million years ago," he said, looking away again. "I was feelin'...shit, it don't matter how I felt. I'm just sorry."

"Oh," I said, cocking my head, surprised. "Thank you."

"It ain't...you're welcome." He took a deep breath and closed his eyes. I wondered what could possibly be on his mind. "Can I walk you to class?"

"Sure," I said, and we fell into step beside each other. He walked beside me in silence for a while, the struggle to say something clear on his features.

"I got a question," he said eventually.

"Shoot."

"What's wrong with me?" Parker said, his voice strangely soft.

"I don't understand," I said.

"What's Grant got that I don't?"

"Ohhhhh." I chewed my lip and looked down at my feet. "I'm not sure I know how to answer that, Parker."

"Was it just 'cause he was the first one to talk to you?" Parker asked earnestly. I shrugged and gave him as tender a look as I could. "How come girls don't like me? How come *you* don't like me?"

"Me and Grant just clicked," I said, "and me and you just…didn't. I don't know how else to explain it." We reached my classroom, and I leaned on the wall to face him. He was still staring straight ahead, and I could see a muscle working in his jaw. "Does that make sense?"

"Yeah," he said eventually. "Yeah, that makes sense."

"This is me," I said, pointing to the chemistry lab I was officially late to now. Parker put his hands in his pockets and started to walk away. "Parker?" I said. He turned, both eyebrows raised. "I'm glad we talked."

He gave me a small smile and nodded before turning away.

CHAPTER
TWENTY-THREE

It was time to find a dress.

I had never bought a dress for homecoming before, of course, and when I suggested we just buy something from Walmart, the very idea nearly drove Layla to hysterics. She insisted that we order our dresses from some website based out of New York she used for all of hers, but it was way too expensive. As a compromise, we drove half an hour south-east to the nearest mall and ventured into JCPenney.

Layla wore a pea coat and opaque Jackie-O glasses, as if afraid someone might see her and undermine her fashionista cred. The rest of us, anticipating a lot of time spent in dressing rooms, had stuck to zip-up hoodies and jeans.

"Let's get something to eat," I announced as we passed through the food court.

"Okay," Layla said grudgingly, "but don't overdo it. And nothing salty! If you get all bloated the dresses won't fit right and you'll end up looking frumpy at homecoming."

"Say it ain't so," Chloe said, pulling out a chair next to me.

"I've been waiting eight years to get you in a dress," Layla said, locking her gaze on Chloe determinedly. "You're in *my* world now."

"Whatever," Chloe replied. "I want Taco Bell."

"I said no salt!" Layla yelled, hurrying after her as she left to get our food.

"You okay?" Anna chirped as she sat across from me.

"Uh, yeah," I said, taking two deep breaths and forcing a smile. This was the first time I had been in a mall since that day in the bathroom, and I was trying not to think about it. "I'm really excited, actually." It wasn't a lie, *really*; I was with my girlfriends, shopping for a dress for an actual dance with my actual boyfriend. I had been excited all the way there, and I would probably be excited again once we were in the store. "You?"

"A little nervous," she said, twisting her fingers in her shimmering curtain of hair and pinching her mouth in worry.

"Your parents?"

"Yeah," Anna said. "I've been skipping lunch for a year, saving the money they give me without them knowing. I feel really bad for lying."

213

I wanted to say, *Your parents are jerks and they don't deserve you*, but what I said instead was, "You're practically eighteen, and it's just a dress."

"It's not, though. You should hear what they say about Layla for wearing clothes that, like, show her *collarbones*." Anna buried her face in her hands and groaned. "This is a mistake. What if they find the dress before homecoming?"

"It's not a mistake," I said. "It's your life and it's your body. Dress it however you want." I caught Chloe coming back with a bag of tacos, Layla following with her shoulders sagging in defeat, and smiled. "And you can keep the dress at my apartment until homecoming."

"Thank you," Anna said with a grateful smile.

"It is literally the least I could do," I said before Chloe and Layla sat down and three out of the four of us dug into our delicious sodium-filled tacos.

"Okay, listen," Layla said, pulling us into a huddle in the middle of the women's section. "This is a *huge* oversimplification but, no offence, I'm starting from square one with you guys. Amanda is a spring, Chloe is an autumn, and Anna, you're a summer."

"I'm also a Scorpio!" I said, giving her a cheesy grin.

"Don't sass me," Layla said, but then paused and added, "Wait, really? Your birthday must be soon."

"You guys know astrology's a form of witchcraft, right?" Anna said, frowning.

"Anna," Layla said, "I love you, but *shush*." She closed her eyes, took a breath, and resumed. "Chloe, the words I want you to keep in mind are 'earth tones'. Stick to greens and browns. You can maybe get away with a blue or a red, but it has to be really muted."

"You can mute colours?" Chloe said.

Layla sighed and turned her attention to Anna next. "Anna, I want you to bring me anything in sort of a light purple – lavender, fuchsia, mauve, you get the idea." Anna nodded seriously and strode off on her tiny legs to begin her quest. "And Amanda, you're looking for jewel tones and sunset colours. Deep sunset colours. Does that make sense?"

"Got it, Coach!" I barked before turning and jogging off into the racks.

"What did I say about sass?" she called after me.

Ten minutes later I arrived at the dressing rooms with a half-dozen options draped over my arm. Chloe shuffled out of one of the stalls looking miserable, swapping a pile of brown and green dresses for another dozen.

I entered a stall adjacent to Chloe's. She just groaned. I stuck my tongue out at an orange dress that had seemed promising on the rack but made me look like a traffic cone.

We were quiet for a moment, me intent on what I was doing and Chloe probably wishing it were spring so she could wear a softball uniform instead. Then she said, "Where were you last weekend? We missed you."

"Last weekend?" I said, my voice cracking a little. I froze in the middle of picking up my last hope – a purple dress with a dramatic cowl neck. "A friend from Atlanta came into town and we hung out..." I paused. I didn't want to lie to her. "With Bee."

"Oh," Chloe said flatly. The purple dress was gorgeous, but somehow I didn't feel as excited any more.

"Chloe—" I began, but she cut me short.

"Don't," she said. "It's fine."

"Chloe, wait," I said as I hurriedly put the dresses back on their hangers and left the dressing room. "I'm Bee's friend too – I have been since before I knew you two were a thing."

"Whatever," Chloe said, emerging from her dressing room. "She likes you, you know."

"What?" I said. "We're friends."

"As more than friends," Chloe said flatly.

"C'mon, Chloe," I said, shaking my head. "She knows I'm straight."

"I've had crushes on straight girls," Chloe mumbled, her voice low enough that it was hard to hear.

"Just...no," I said, shaking my head to dispel the thought. "We're *just* friends, Chloe. And we were just hanging out. It didn't occur to me it would hurt you at the time," I said.

"Well, it did." She looked so lonely all of a sudden, standing there under the fluorescent light, next to that pile of rumpled dresses. I moved towards her, wanting to hug her but unsure if she would let me, when Layla rounded the corner, hangers dangling from her hands.

"Whoa!" she cried, grabbing my arm and pulling me towards the mirror, taking in the purple dress. "Spin," she ordered, and I obliged.

"Does the cowl neck make my shoulders look too big?" I asked as I came to a stop. I gazed at my profile in the mirror, grateful to have somewhere to look other than Chloe's hurt gaze.

"No, it *minimizes* the shoulders," Layla said with an eye-roll, but she was smiling. "Honestly, it's like starting from scratch with you two. I ought to teach a class called 'How to Be a Girl'." She grabbed my discarded dresses to return them, and Chloe retreated back into her dressing room.

I stood there for a moment, staring at the closed door, Layla's words ringing in my ears. I had never been good at being a boy, and I didn't enjoy it very much, but there were parts to it that made a certain kind of sense – when boys were angry, they showed it with their fists, and then it was done. With girls, I knew, it was different. I had hurt Chloe without even realizing it, and unlike a bruise, it would take more than a few days to go away.

CHAPTER
TWENTY-FOUR

"Happy birthday!" Layla grinned and waved from the booth she shared with Chloe a few days later.

"Thanks," I said as I sat down next to Chloe. She offered me a small smile. We still hadn't talked much since our fight in the dressing room, but it felt like the hurt was fading. Eventually, I hoped, there would be no sign it had been there at all.

"So how's it feel being eighteen?" Anna asked. I froze, remembering that they didn't know about my year off. I'd already been eighteen a year, but there was no way to explain the truth. It was strange to have such normal friendships for the first time, but still have so many secrets.

"Yeah," Layla said. "Have you bought cigarettes yet?"

"I don't smoke," I said with a shrug, my stomach twisting from yet another half-truth. Smoking cigarettes on my hormones could cause fatal blood clots, but I couldn't tell them about that either.

"Neither do I," Layla said, waving dismissively. "It's about the milestone. Which reminds me…" She reached under the table and brought out a small present wrapped in silvery paper.

"We all chipped in," Anna said, practically bouncing in her seat.

"You guys!" I said, a surge of emotion overcoming me as I untied the ribbon. "You didn't have to."

"Did anyway," Chloe said. I looked over at her, trying to catch her gaze. I wanted to make sure everything was back to normal after our conversation at the mall, but as always her expression was unreadable. "Happy birthday."

I opened the box and lifted out a pair of lovely amethyst stud earrings that matched my homecoming dress perfectly, glimmering in the late-morning sun. "I love them!" I said, then added sadly. "But my ears aren't pierced."

"We know. We're getting them pierced," Anna said brightly. "We promised Grant we'd keep you busy while he got your present ready."

"Wait, what?" I said. "What is it?"

"Don't change the subject." Layla steepled her fingers like a super-villain. "And trust me, it's best if you come quietly."

* * *

The Rebel Yell tattoo parlour was a small cube of brick sitting in a rutted gravel parking lot. As we entered, a happy little bell chimed, just barely audible over Molly Hatchet blasting at full volume.

"Hey, Riley!" Layla called. A rail-thin girl with shorn green hair and gauges in her ears crushed Layla in a hug.

"This is my cousin Riley," Layla said, smiling, an arm around the girl's shoulder. "She's basically the biggest badass ever."

"Naw," Riley said, smiling back. She turned to face us. "So who's today's victim?"

"Right here," Layla said, hooking her arm around mine, "Amanda."

"Nice to meet you, Amanda. You'll be with Rod today – he'll take good care of you." Riley yelled across the tattoo parlour and a man with a shaved head and flannel shirt came over.

"Hey there." Rod smiled, motioning to the chair. "Whatcha interested in? Upper cartilage, maybe get a gauge started?"

"Oh, no," Layla said. "Her ears aren't pierced at all."

"A virgin!" Rod said, smiling. I felt my cheeks flush. "Well, don't worry, y'all came to the right place. I know it's probably a little intimidating in here, but we'll take good care of you."

Layla eyed my nervous face. She pointed at me and then pointed at the chair. I gripped the armrests like I was riding a roller coaster and closed my eyes, trying to keep my breathing under control.

"Don't tell me when it's coming," I said, listening to the crinkle of plastic as Rod unwrapped the needle. I focused on happy things instead – how just this moment, the boy of my dreams was preparing a birthday surprise, how friends who knew me well were dead set on getting me what I wanted, and not taking no for an answer. I couldn't remember the last time I'd wanted to celebrate my birthday, but for the first time in a long time, I felt like I had something to celebrate. "Do something to distract me."

"Okay," Layla said, sounding mischievous. A quiet moment passed, and then she said, "You know how Anna and me are on the homecoming committee?"

"Yeah?"

"Well, we nominated you for homecoming queen!"

I didn't even notice when the needle went in.

CHAPTER
TWENTY-FIVE

My ears still stung when the girls dropped me off near the trail to the tree house. I knew better than to try to find out from them what Grant had planned, so I got out of the car without protest, smiling to myself as Layla wolf-whistled and screeched down the street. Once they were out of sight I made my way down the trail, my hoodie providing minimal protection against the chill blowing off the lake.

The undergrowth was mostly dead this far into November, and layers of fallen leaves obscured the path. I heard distant music and followed it to its source. When I stepped out of the trees I got my first glimpse of the lake glittering like crystal in the late afternoon sun. It took me a moment to realize that Grant was there, leaning against the tree, fiddling absent-mindedly with a lighter.

He wore a slightly threadbare black suit with buttons

that shimmered in the light. His hair was combed and slicked back, and he had shaved. I loved the feel of his stubble on my face, but his smooth cheeks made him look princely and dashing. I took a small step forward.

"Wow," I said. "I mean, hi. Apparently you've been getting something ready?" I recognized the music as the soundtrack to *Amélie* and grinned.

"Your birthday present," he said, rubbing the back of his neck and smiling sheepishly. He nodded towards the ladder. I climbed up and saw the tree house floor covered in a white blanket, with two plates of food. Candles flickered on the window ledge. "Surprise!"

I hugged him and gave him a kiss.

"What's that smell?" I said. "It's wonderful."

"Sole Meunière," Grant said. "Hope I pronounced that right." He hadn't, but he had got it wrong in a cute way. "And there's a hot potato salad and some baked zucchini with olive oil too." He laced his fingers in mine and I felt so good, like lying in a sunbeam on a spring afternoon and falling into cold water after exercising all at once. "I remembered what you said when we watched *Amélie*, about wanting to live in Paris one day, so I thought I'd bring France here for a night."

"Grant," I said, turning to him, "this is wonderful. I don't know what to say."

"Yeah," Grant said. I realized he was staring at me. "You make me feel that way a lot." His lips parted as we stared at each other, and for a moment our eyes just danced back and forth and we breathed each other in.

He stepped forward and pressed his lips to mine. I closed my eyes and leaned into him, my fingertips grazing the lapels of his jacket as our mouths moved. I smiled and bit his lip as I undid the buttons on his jacket. He shrugged it off and broke our kiss to gingerly hang his jacket over a tree branch.

"Sorry," he said. "It's just it's the only suit I've got and I don't wanna mess it up. It needs to last me at least until homecoming."

I silently hooked a finger around his tie and pulled him to the tree trunk. He fussed at first, afraid the food might get cold, but I wasn't hungry. I untied his tie, throwing it onto the same branch as his jacket. He placed his hand on my thigh. I put my hand against his chest and loved how hard his muscles were under his shirt, and especially how different our bodies were, how we were as different as two people could be but when he kissed me again our differences came together and we weren't hard chest muscles or a soft thigh or breasts or beard shadow, we were just one thing exploring itself and shivering with the joy of it.

He reached under my skirt and I stiffened instinctively, still not used to that territory being safe. He looked up at me, eyes wide, and I slowly loosened back up. I nodded and we resumed our kiss as his fingers danced up my thigh and found the top of my leggings, which he slowly pulled down. We both looked at my legs as he unpeeled them. They were November pale, but long and shapely. Seeing him see them, I loved them even more. He ran his hand up my calf to the back of my knee and then up the back of my thigh and I gasped at the realization that touch could be like this. I thought of that poor girl pretending to be a boy who tried to kill herself and I wanted her to see this, to feel this, so she could understand that one day she might not just be okay with her body but that she would be able to feel things, beautiful things, inside of it.

He kissed the nape of my neck and I unbuttoned his shirt and slid it down his arms. His body was so lean and strong and real, not the body of a model or a movie star or even really an athlete, but a body with muscles built from long, tiring labour. I lifted my sweater over my head and I wasn't afraid. I wasn't afraid. We stared at each other for a moment and came to a silent decision. I stood and wiggled out of my skirt while he sat forward and shucked his trousers. We looked at each other again, and my breath caught in my chest.

I bit my lip and unclasped my bra and let it fall to the floor. His eyes were so wide I could see my reflection in them, and the girl in those mirrors was smiling and she was beautiful. He took me by the arms and pulled me back down. I giggled and ran my fingers down his stomach as he crawled on top of me.

He kissed me again and I wrapped my arms around him. His fingers ran down my side, tickling me, and it took every ounce of willpower not to giggle and squirm, and from there they passed over my hip bone and down further still. I didn't stop him but I breathed in sharply and stiffened. His eyes snapped open and he raised himself off me, his eyes wide with concern.

"Is this your first time?" he asked. When I looked away, he touched my cheek, turning my gaze back to his. "Of course it's your first time. You said I was your first kiss. Sorry."

"It's okay," I said, biting my lip. I knew where I wanted to go with Grant tonight, but now that we were here, I was scared.

"Okay." He rolled onto his side and rested his hand on my cheek. "Do you wanna slow down?"

"Yeah," I said, grateful that he knew, and understood. "This is really wonderful, but yeah."

"That's fine," he said. "That's so absolutely fine." He rolled onto his back. We laced our fingers together and watched the sky fade from orange to purple to black, just feeling each other's warmth and listening to each other's breathing.

"I've been thinking about the future," Grant said. I turned to look at him. He was still staring up at the dome of stars above us. "I can't get into NYU or anything, but I talked to the guidance counsellor and she said if I get my

226

grades up I could get some grants and go to college in state. I might be able to go to community college without even takin' out any loans."

"Wow," I said, snuggling up next to him and resting a hand over his heart. It was beating so fast. I didn't ask what he was going to do about his family – I wanted him to only think about himself, for once.

"And I was thinkin'," he said, turning now to look at me. Our noses pressed together and I unfocused my eyes. "I could use some of my financial aid and get a computer, and when you're in New York we could Skype each other."

"Maybe you could come up and visit," I said.

"Maybe," Grant said. "That'd be nice."

"And maybe," I said, bringing my lips close to his and letting my eyelids droop, "once you've got all A's down here, you could transfer to my school and get an apartment with me."

"For now though," he said, pulling me tight to him and sneaking a quick kiss, "this is just fine."

I nodded. But my mind was already racing ahead, imagining a future I had scarcely allowed myself to consider. I thought of Grant holding my hand as we walked down a New York City street, of lounging on a blanket in Central Park, reading for class as he napped peacefully beside me. I knew we were only just beginning, but I couldn't help imagining what it would be like to be with him until the end.

"I want you to be my first," I said, chewing the inside of my cheek. "When I'm ready, I want it to be you."

"No rush," Grant said, burying his face in my shoulder. "We've got all the time in the world."

AUGUST, TWO YEARS AGO

"You really wanna come?" Mom called from the living room. "Pretty sure I know what you like by now."

"I haven't left the house all summer," I called back. I accidentally turned my head as I spoke, smearing a line of eyeliner from the middle of my eyelid up to my eyebrow.

"Shit." I took a deep breath and closed my eyes, trying to stay calm. This should have been easy. I'd been drawing and painting since I was in kindergarten. But nothing was easy, not in this strange in-between time. The hormones I'd been taking hadn't finished their work yet, and I wouldn't be old enough for the surgery until next summer.

I opened my eyes and looked in the mirror sitting on my desk. My hair was still short and boyish, though its growth had sped up noticeably thanks to the hormones. My right eye was bare while my left eye was ringed with eyeshadow and eyeliner in thick, childish smears.

My cheeks were two bright, red circles like an embarrassed anime character. I watched as my mouth screwed up and my eyes started to twitch. I felt tears forming, and I knew that if I let them loose I would have to start all over, but I felt so helpless and stupid that I wondered what the point was in the first place. Mom knocked gently at my door.

"I changed my mind," I said. I tried to sound calm but it came out as a pathetic whimper.

"You're crying."

"I'm f-fine."

"You can't lie to me," she said. "You got ten seconds before I come in there, so if you need to make yourself decent, now's the time."

I shuffled over to my bed and slouched on the edge, still sniffling. My cat, Guinevere, padded across the bed and bopped her face into my shoulder, the sound of her purring only just barely lifting my spirits. The door creaked. I watched Mom's white sandals as she came in. She sat down beside me and her soft, round hand squeezed my shoulder.

"I look stupid," I said. "I'm not a boy or a girl any more. I'm just broken. It would have been easier if I'd died."

"Easier for who?" Mom said. Her hand tightened. I turned to face her and there was a steeliness in her narrowed eyes that seemed completely out of place in her soft features.

"Everybody but you I guess," I whispered. I looked away again and her grip weakened.

"You wouldn't hurt your mama, right?"

"Right," I muttered.

"You promise you ain't gonna…again…?"

"Promise."

"Atta girl," she said. She grabbed both shoulders and turned me towards her, looking all roses and biscuits again. "Mason girls don't quit."

"I'm still a Hardy."

"Well, your dad's mama was a hard old bitch, so she counts too." I smiled despite myself. "Now, let's see what all the fuss is about." She put her fingers under my chin and turned my face this way and that, a thoughtful expression on her face. "Good lord, Amanda, you got a good inch slathered on here. Who said you needed this much?"

"The internet," I said sheepishly. Mom made a dubious noise at the back of her throat.

"The internet says lots of things, hon. Remember Hank?"

"The ointment guy?"

"Yup. internet said we was a perfect match, and look how that turned out. Ointment stains in my damn carpet and just as single as ever."

I laughed, forgetting the burning puffiness around my eyes for a moment. She grabbed the make-up wipes off my desk and started gently rubbing my face like she used to when I was little. "Make-up has lotsa uses. One of 'em

231

is to highlight your eyes, cheeks and lips so they stick out a little, give you a kinda feminine glow that boys think's natural. There now."

"What are the other uses?"

"Looking young," she said without looking up. "But if you looked any younger, folks'd wonder why I let you out of your crib."

I laughed. This felt right. This felt like the moment I had wanted with Mom since I was old enough to know I wanted anything at all.

"Quit moving! Now, wink at me and hold it." I did as I was told. The tip of her tongue poked out of her lips and she squinted as she took the pencil to my eyelid in long, graceful strokes. "Now, open both eyes and look up."

She ran the pencil along the waterline of both eyes. "You know I thought you were gonna be a girl when I was pregnant?" My eyebrows popped up. She snorted and made a tutting sound, and I forced myself to return to a neutral expression. "I was a little sad when you came out a boy. I knew I didn't wanna go through that whole ordeal again, so I was afraid I'd never get to show anybody this stuff."

"Me too," I said. I closed my eyes as she lightly brushed a peach blush onto my cheeks. "I was afraid too, I mean."

"You still afraid?" she said. I opened my eyes and saw a look of concern pulling her smile down.

"Yeah," I said. "Not as much. In different ways. Scared

of getting hurt by people instead of scared to live at all."

"At least you're smart as I always thought then," she said. "Pucker up. Being a girl in this world means being afraid. That fear'll keep you safe. It'll keep you alive."

"Is it really that bad?"

She ran the balm along my lips and signalled for me to pucker. "Maybe not. Who knows? World's different now. When you told me about…your condition, I was more sad for you for having to deal with being a girl than anything else. Go check your reflection."

"Oh," I said when I reached the mirror. I brushed my fingers against the glass. Burgundy lines around my eyes, faint peach pigment on my cheekbones, and brownish-red lip gloss, and somehow the face staring out at me was one I'd never seen before. It was the one I always felt like I should have seen.

A wave of vertigo washed over me. I leaned back against the wall and grabbed a nearby bookshelf. My cheeks hurt and my eyes were starting to water again, but it felt different.

"You okay?" Mom said, walking up behind me.

"I think I might be allergic or something. I feel kinda strange…sort of floaty and light-headed."

"You ain't sick, hon," Mom said. She kissed my cheek and hugged me so tight I thought I might break a rib. "That's joy."

CHAPTER
TWENTY-SIX

"Have fun tonight," Dad said as we pulled into the school parking lot. The homecoming game had ended hours before, with the team pulling out a fourth-quarter victory, and I was hoarse but happy from cheering Grant on from the stands. I wore the knee-length purple dress with a cowl neck, the amethyst earrings the girls had bought me for my birthday, and low gold heels. In them I would be Grant's height or a little taller, but for once I didn't care.

"Thanks for the ride," I said, reaching for the door handle. I had got distracted when Anna stopped by to pick up her dress, then spent too long on my hair and make-up, and now I was late meeting Grant, the girls and their dates for photos on the school lawn – a Lambertville High tradition, apparently.

"Amanda, wait," Dad said as I got out of the car.

His tone was serious, and I worried he was going to give me another lecture about being careful.

"I've got to go," I told him. I could see Anna bounding towards me across the parking lot, waving.

"I just wanted to tell you," Dad began, stuttering and awkward. He didn't look at me as he said, "You look really beautiful tonight."

"Oh," I said. "Thank you." My face flushed.

"And be safe," I heard him call behind me as I got out and closed the door, but it felt like an instinct, like something all fathers said to their daughters.

"Amanda!" Anna cried as I got out of the car, coming towards me with a broad, mischievous smile. "Amanda, look! Chloe's wearing a dress."

I turned towards the school lawn, where the setting sun had cast everything in a warm, golden glow, and saw Chloe in a red sleeveless dress that matched the colour of her hair – just the shade that Layla had advised. I marvelled at how lean and well-muscled her arms were and how lovely she was with her hair straightened and a hint of make-up on her eyes and cheeks – or how lovely she *would* have looked if she weren't scowling and shuffling her feet like a sullen toddler. I knew the feeling, of course, since that was how I'd felt every day I'd had to wear boys' clothes.

"Shut up," Chloe said.

Grant arrived a few minutes later, his suit crisp and clean. He whistled when he saw me, his eyes wide and appreciative, and I had never felt more beautiful. I kissed him, and then we lined up for pictures, our arms wrapped like ribbons around the best present ever, and smiled so much our cheeks hurt.

The homecoming committee, under Anna and Layla's expert guidance, had taken the "Heroes' Homecoming" theme and transformed our drab, run-down gym into something out of *The Odyssey*. Canvases painted with profiles of Greek heroes slaying monsters lined the walls, hiding the folded-up bleachers. The ceiling was covered in blue streamers interspersed with hanging cardboard hydras and sea monsters. The DJ onstage at the far end of the gym even wore a toga.

I pulled Grant into the centre of the crowd and danced with him as "All Night" by Icona Pop blared over the speakers. Something resonated in me whenever the singer declared, "We got the keys to open paradise," and I felt too miraculous not to be moving with the boy I liked so much. I pulled him close, buried my face in his neck, and breathed him in, and realized I didn't *like* him.

I loved him. I loved him, I knew that now. I tried to tell him, but the noise silenced my words. He cocked his head, and I just laughed and kissed him. There would be time to talk later. I thought of what he had said the other night, *We have all the time in the world*. We danced to song after song, my hair loose from my careful updo plastered with sweat against my forehead and my new heels digging into my feet, but I didn't care. Finally, we were too worn out to continue. I kissed Grant and excused myself to the bathroom.

The halls felt like a crypt after the humidity in the gym. My clicking steps echoed off the rows of lockers and the chilly air raised goosebumps on my arms. I opened the bathroom door and paused when I saw Bee leaning against the sink with her eyes closed.

"Oh, hey!" I said.

She smiled and swayed in place. Her eyes were red and her cheeks were bright pink.

"Hi," she said, slurring just a little.

"You okay?"

"Yeah," she said. She blinked a few times, laughed, and leaned against the sink. "Yeah I'm fine. Are *you* fine though?"

"Of course," I said, wrapping her in a hug. She sank into my arms and sighed happily, then pushed me out to arm's length and stared into my eyes.

"But are you fine?" Bee said. "Are you really?"

"Why wouldn't I be?" I said.

"Does Grant know yet?" She looked around for a moment and then added in a loud whisper, "About – you know."

"No…" I said, confused. We hadn't talked about my secret since Virginia had come to town, and I wondered what was on her mind. "I tried to tell him, but he said he didn't need to know. Why?"

"You need to be with somebody who can share everything," she said in a rush, and I could tell she'd been thinking about saying this for a long time. I suddenly remembered what Chloe had told me in the mall. "You're so interesting and complicated—"

"Thanks, but—"

"And Grant's so basic and normal." She swayed and poked a finger into my chest. "That's your problem. You work so, so hard to be *boring* so you can impress *boring* people."

"I don't," I said, my stomach twisting.

"That's not true," Bee said, shaking her head. And then she reached out, took the front of my dress, and pulled me into a kiss before I could stop her. I pulled back immediately.

"What the hell, Bee?" I said, my voice tilting up shrilly. "What was that?"

"Oh, come on," Bee said. Her cheeks were so red they practically glowed. "You've convinced yourself and everybody else that you're this perfect, demure girl next door when you could be so much more."

"Maybe I am the girl next door," I said angrily. Bee pursed her lips and twitched like I'd hit her. I realized that under the bravado and the alcohol was a girl who had just made herself vulnerable and been shot down. I took a deep breath and softened my voice. "Listen, Bee, I'm really sorry if I gave you the impression—"

"Of *course* you're sorry!"

"If I gave you the impression," I said, going on, "that we were ever a possibility. But I like boys. I only like boys." She stared at her feet in silence for a moment, her whole face going from pink to red. She sniffled once, and I thought she might be about to cry, but then she looked up and I didn't see any tears. "Bee—" I went on, wanting to smooth things over between us, but was interrupted by the bathroom door flying open and Anna rushing in.

"There you are!" she cried, grabbing my arm. "We've been looking everywhere for you!"

"Give us a minute? We were just—" I tried to protest, but Anna was already ushering me towards the door.

I gave Bee a last look as we left, hoping things between us would be okay. "What's going on?" I asked Anna, but she just shook her head, and I knew enough from the ear-piercing kidnapping not to ask any more questions.

"There she is!" Layla cried as we came through the gym's double doors and the spotlight fell on me. My eyes adjusted to the light and I realized everyone had turned to look at me. Grant appeared by my side on the gym floor and clutched my hand, smiling like a little boy. "You missed the announcement!"

"What announcement?" I said, my voice feeling strangely loud in the suddenly quiet gym.

"Homecoming queen!" Layla cried. She held out a silvery tiara that glinted in the light and hopped down from the stage. It took her a long time to get to me; when she finally broke through the crowd and wove the tiara into my hair my heart was beating so fast I thought I might die. She hugged me, whispered "Congratulations" in my ear, and she and Grant brought me back to an empty circle in the middle of the crowd. Music started playing, but I didn't hear it. I just saw smiling faces pointed at me in every direction, Grant's the brightest of them, and I felt myself in my own body being loved and accepted, and it felt so good it was almost surreal. This wasn't my life. This couldn't be my life. Things like this *did not* happen to girls like me.

I was drawn back to reality by Bee's voice, just barely audible, yelling over the crowd and the music. Everyone turned towards the stage, a look of confusion on the faces around me. There was Bee, swaying badly, blinking glassy eyes against the stage lights as she grabbed the mike.

"Hi," she said. We all winced at a sudden screech of feedback. "Yay home team! Sports!" She stumbled but quickly caught herself and looked straight down at her feet. "Wooooo football yay!"

"She's wasted," Grant said. I wrapped my arms around his and looked around the gym. The reactions in the sea of faces were mixed, some angry, some confused, some laughing. I saw the chaperones panicking and one of them heading towards the stage from all the way across the gym.

"Hey, I don't have long," Bee said, waving to the oncoming chaperone, "so I'll get to it. I hate this fuckin' town, I hate this school, and I hate all of you, and do you know why? I hate y'all because you could be so great. So many of you are, like, one step away from being so cool, and you're so afraid of *nothing* that you all pretend to be normal." A ball of ice began to form in my stomach. I hugged Grant's arm tighter and he kissed me just above my ear.

"Well, that's over tonight. Callie's had two abortions!" she cried, pointing at a heavyset girl near the stage. "Austin's a fag!" she declared, turning to point at a shaggy-haired boy I didn't know standing by himself near the punch.

People were beginning to whisper. People were beginning to look afraid.

Bee started looking around the gym rapid-fire. "Fucking the science teacher! Drug dealer!"

Her finger landed on Chloe, who glanced up and scowled when she heard her name. "Dyke!" Bee cried. The chaperone had been slowed by the crush of people near the stage but he was close now, almost at the stairs. Bee pointed at herself and yelled, "Queer! Slut!"

And then she pointed at me.

"But I saved the best for last, y'all," she said. "Look at our homecoming queen. Ain't she sweet? Ain't she beautiful?

241

She's livin' the dream, right? I bet a lot of you guys've thought about her in the shower. Smart, pretty, but not pushy or intimidating…she's everything this fucked-up place wants a girl to be." The chaperone was mounting the steps. I couldn't stop shaking. Grant held me close and in that moment I loved him so much. "But guys, guess what: she's a *he*!" The crowd went silent, the only noise the sound of the scuffle as the chaperone finally made it to the stage and grabbed the mike from Bee.

A few people looked confused, but most laughed it off. As eyes turned to me I realized my hands were shaking. People started whispering to each other. Grant looked over at me, seeming unfazed by what he assumed was some kind of bizarre prank, and then he saw the haunted look on my face.

"Oh my God," Grant said as the realization dawned on him, a look of absolute confusion and horror in his eyes. I wanted to say something, to pause and give us time, to stop the next few minutes from happening like I knew they would, but I couldn't.

I ran.

CHAPTER
TWENTY-SEVEN

"**A**manda, wait!" Grant said. I barely even registered that I was hearing him until he grabbed my arm and stopped me just short of the gym's double doors. I struggled for a moment and then turned to face him.

"It's not true, right?" Grant said, letting go of my arm. "It's just a prank you two came up with when y'all were stoned?"

"You promised you wouldn't ever hate me," I whispered, looking at his chest. Somehow that seemed to be enough of an answer for him. Muscles in his jaw jumped and twitched and I could actually hear the grinding of his teeth. "You promised you'd never regret being with me."

"*What?*" Grant said, stepping forward. I stepped back and nearly stumbled, feeling sick to my stomach. Tears welled in his eyes. "You're a *boy?* I remember what I fucking said, but how can you be a boy?"

"I'm not," I said, my voice still low and soft, and for the first time I noticed the crowd behind us, listening intently. "I was..." I swallowed. "I was born a boy." We were both quiet for a moment.

"What?" Grant said, his voice rising. "What does that *mean?* Do you...do you have a penis?"

"Do I?" I croaked. "I feel like you would've noticed."

"I don't know how this shit works," Grant said, his shoulders sagging, "and you keep giving me half answers. Do you have one or not?"

"What's it matter?" I snapped, finally meeting his gaze. Now it was his turn to back away from me. "What's between my legs is officially not your business any more, right?"

"Okay," Grant said, and my heart broke when he didn't argue. "But what's that say about me then? Does that—" He took a breath and slowed down, saying, "Does this make me gay?"

"No," I said quietly. "How nice for you."

He noticed the people gathered around us for the first time and his face went pale. He started to say something else but I just shook my head. I wanted to be alone, in the quiet, perhaps on the wet grass outside so I could stare up at the autumn sky and lie down and feel nothing until eventually my body slipped into the earth and nothing became everything.

I turned to face the crowd. Some of them had their hands over their mouths, eyebrows floating high on their foreheads. They were all staring silently, my friends included. I realized I was still wearing the tiara Layla had hooked into my hair and I unwound it. Up close, it looked tacky and cheap and stupid.

"Here," I said, tossing the tiara so that it skittered to a stop at Layla's feet. She stooped and picked it up, looking from the crown back to me slowly. "I guess I'm disqualified."

I turned before anyone could say anything and hurried out of the school and into the night.

CHAPTER
TWENTY-EIGHT

I ran down the side of the highway as if possessed. My feelings were pouring off me like sweat, like the colour sloughing off a painting drenched in turpentine. A semi honked loudly as it thundered by. I cried out in surprise and tumbled to the ground, twisting my ankle. My vision swam from the pain but I took my heels off, stood up, and kept limping.

My feet were freezing and my ankle throbbed every time I put weight on it. I looked up and saw the stars wheeling overhead, absolutely clear and present in air this cold, this far from light pollution. Last time I had come this way the heat had nearly beaten me, and the overgrown weeds had lashed at my calves while the cicadas watched and screamed, but now the cold was seeping into my feet and the wet was clinging to my dress and the stars were watching, disinterested.

I heard the absurdly celebratory *Star Wars* theme from deep in my purse and looked at my phone. Dad was calling – had called a bunch of times. Word must have already spread around town. I looked up from my purse and saw that a truck had pulled onto the shoulder a little way away. I blinked against the glare of the headlights and held up a hand to shield my eyes.

"Hey beautiful," Parker said as he pulled forward, his truck tyres crunching the gravel like bone. The cab was pitch black for a moment while my eyes adjusted, but then I could just barely make out his face in the darkness. "Need a ride?"

"I'm fine," I said, trying to speed up. His truck kept up with me easily and after thirty seconds of a near-normal walking pace I had to hiss in pain and stop to rub my throbbing ankle.

"I see you limpin', *bro*," he said, the last word hitting me like a punch in the stomach. I squared my shoulders and limped at a more tolerable pace.

"Please don't call me that," I said.

"Why not?" he said. I noticed his voice sounded strange. "Ain't you Grant's little boyfriend? And since I'm Grant's friend, that makes us bros."

"I'm not his boyfriend," I said, turning and glaring at his silhouette.

"Right, right," Parker said, "'cause he dumped you, I heard."

"No," I said, my stomach churning from shame and anger and pain. "I was never his boyfriend."

"Well, what were you then?" he said. "'Cause you're not a girl."

"Whatever, Parker," I said through clenched teeth. The hairs on the back of my neck were standing on end and I felt the metallic edge of panic in my blood, but I kept walking.

"Aw, I didn't mean that," Parker said. "I mean, sure, technically, no, you sure as hell ain't a girl, but you *look* like one at least."

"Okay," I said, swallowing and glancing at him again. I thought I saw a flash of reflected light from his eyes in the darkness. He laughed, suddenly and loudly, making me jump and catch my breath.

"Relax!" he said. "I'm just fuckin' with you. Now, hop in and lemme give you a ride."

"Parker, please," I said, "just keep driving. I don't want a ride."

"Oh, you want a ride," Parker said, and as my eyes readjusted to the darkness I saw he was smiling wide but his nostrils were flared and his eyebrows were knotting together. "You just don't want a ride from me."

"I want to be left alone," I said.

Another text from Dad bathed the inside of my bag in a blue glow for a moment and I remembered my phone. I pulled it out of my purse and tried to unlock it when the truck's engine suddenly died and Parker jumped out. His huge hand clamped over my wrist. I looked up at him, wide-eyed, and slowly dropped my phone back into my purse.

"That's better," he said, letting go of my wrist. "Like hell you wanna be left alone. If you wanted to be left alone you'd've stayed a boy."

"What are you doing?" I said.

"Walkin' with you," he said, easily keeping pace with me, his shoulders hunched forward and his hands in his pockets. I smelled something sour and sterile wafting off him and realized he had been drinking. "It's dangerous out here. Don't worry though, I'll keep you safe."

"Okay," I said, wrapping my arms around myself and looking off into the darkness between the trees. His shadow stretched out past mine. I remembered Mom telling me how frightening men were, all men really, how helpless it often felt to be a woman among men, and for the first time I understood what she meant.

I reached into my bag again, my fingers curled around my phone, when the punch came. Something thudded against the side of my skull as the dark around me turned red and all the night sounds of the road were replaced by a ringing in my right ear. I stumbled like a drunk away from the road until I scraped my bare shoulder against a tree and clung to it. Parker was on me before I could fully grasp what had happened, his face inches from mine and his forearm braced against my throat, cutting off just enough of my oxygen that I started to gag and see stars.

"No," Parker hissed, "that's not how this works. You made me look like a dickhead for months, and now you don't got Grant to look out for you. You don't get to play hard to get any more." I could barely hear him, and his features were blacked out by the bright headlights of his truck. I tried to speak but all that came out was a gagging sound. "You coulda had this the easy way. Now, let's see how close you are to the real thing."

The sensation of his huge hands pulling up the hem of my dress brought me just far enough from my stupor to act. I let out a screaming croak and clawed at his face as I drove my knee into his crotch as hard as I could. He coughed loudly and went limp. I was still woozy and disoriented, but some animal part of my brain forced me to act. I lurched into the darkness and the underbrush, keeping one eye over my shoulder as I ran into the woods.

Parker stomped after me, snapping branches and growling my name. The dots in my eyes and the ringing in my ears made it impossible to figure out how near or far he was, but after a few minutes I heard the crunch of gravel again and the sweep of a new set of headlights followed by the sound of slamming car doors and female voices ahead.

I slowly, carefully, started creeping my way towards the road. I was about halfway there when my busted ankle slipped out from under me. I reached out to grab another branch for support, only to have it snap loudly as I cried out and fell to the wet ground.

"Found you!" Parker yelled. I tried to stand but he was bursting through the darkness in seconds, pouncing on me and pushing me down into the mud with a horrible, irresistible strength. I heard something rip as the left strap of my dress fell loose. I kicked and slapped at him but my feet couldn't get to him and he quickly pinned my wrists down by my head. He had just kicked my knees apart when I heard a metallic *click* from behind him.

"I knew you were a creep," a girl's voice said. A beam of light landed on us, revealing Chloe's silhouette holding a rifle pointed at Parker's back.

Parker slowly stood. I scrambled backwards until my head hit a tree trunk and pulled my knees to myself, gasping. Chloe led Parker away, leaving me in darkness again until a small hand grasped mine and pulled me up.

"Come on," Anna said, her voice hushed.

We made it to the road, where I saw Parker standing with his hands pressed to his truck, his face red as tendons jumped in his jaw. Chloe stood vigilant behind him, her hunting rifle still raised, a look of absolute, dispassionate boredom on her face.

"We've got her," I heard Layla say, sounding calm but with an undercurrent of panic. "I'll call you back." I turned and saw her putting her phone away as she jogged over to us. She pulled me into a hug and I winced at a burning pain in my shoulder and ribs. "We were so worried!"

"I'm fine," I said. "Thank you."

"Grant texted us," Layla said, leaning in to examine my face and making a pained expression.

"Yeah," Anna said. "He said Parker'd called him once word started getting around. Said he sounded drunk, talkin' about helpin' Grant get revenge on you and putting you in your place."

"Oh," I said, pulling on the strap of my dress. I was shivering even though I didn't feel cold. I didn't feel much of anything. "That was nice of him."

"Amanda?" Layla said, taking my hand and giving me a worried look. "You okay?"

"No," I said, realizing for the first time just how badly I was shaking.

"Want us to call the police?" Anna said. I looked over my shoulder and saw Chloe watching me, both eyebrows raised.

"Do you want to go to the hospital?" Layla added.

"No," I said.

The last thing I wanted was for a nurse to take pictures of me. The last thing I wanted was a night spent with police officers who had probably already heard about me by now, and wanted to ask questions about my private parts instead of about what had happened. I just wanted to forget everything about tonight. I wanted it to be over.

Chloe prodded Parker once with the rifle and barked for him to leave. He complied quickly, jumping into his truck and driving off into the night.

"If you say so," Layla said. She was quiet for a moment, then looked right into my eyes. "What *can* we do?"

"Please just take me home," I said.

CHAPTER
TWENTY-NINE

I laid my head against the passenger window as Layla drove silently. The chilly glass was a relief on the throbbing skin where Parker's punch had landed. I closed my left eye – the right was already swelling shut – and willed myself through time. I wanted this car ride to be over. I wanted to skip the conversation with Dad and the bus ride back to Atlanta and Mom's worried looks and just be back in my room in Smyrna with the blackout curtains pulled tight.

"I owe you an apology," Layla said. I glanced in her direction but didn't say anything. "I'm sorry we just stood there, in the gym."

"It's okay," I said. "I wouldn't know how to handle me if I were you."

"That's not even it," Layla said, shaking her head. "It's—"

"Don't lie to me, okay?" I said louder than I meant to, making a cutting motion with my hand. "Thanks for what you did with Parker, but you can stop pretending."

"Amanda…"

"I'm a *freak*," I said. Tears came but I wasn't sad. I thought maybe I was angry, but I didn't know who I was angry at. Grant, for not loving me. Parker, for what he had done. My dad for warning me, for being right. Myself maybe, for thinking I could ever be happy. "I'm a freak, and jerks like Parker are always going to want to see the freak show, as long as they know the truth about me."

"Amanda!" Layla said. I sniffled and scowled at her, but the look she gave me withered my anger. "Don't you dare talk about my friend that way." She reached out and grabbed my left hand with her right. I flinched at the touch but quickly accepted it. "The *truth* is that you're my friend, Amanda. You're one of the most beautiful girls I've ever known, inside and out."

"Really?" I said, wiping my nose.

"Hell yeah," Layla said. "I mean, I'm trying to picture what you must've been like before you became Amanda, and I can't even think of a way the Amanda I know could ever pull off being a boy."

"I wasn't very good at it," I said, a small smile twitching at my mouth. Layla smiled in return.

"Listen," she said, after a short silence fell between us. "We love you no matter what."

"I love you guys too." I smiled, and my bruised temple throbbed painfully.

We pulled into my apartment complex. I thanked her again and started to get out, but she squeezed my hand and gave me a serious look.

"You don't have to go in," she said. "You can come stay with me tonight."

"No," I said, taking my hand from hers and giving her a reassuring smile. "Thank you, but no. I'm feeling better."

"Okay," Layla said. "I'm gonna wait out here for half an hour though. If you feel like you need to be around friends, just come on out and we'll have a sleepover."

I thanked Layla again and limped up the stairs, dreading the coming conversation with Dad. I reached our door and started to turn the knob when it was yanked open from within. Dad stood in the doorway, his shoulders squared and his expression full of worry.

"Oh my God," he said, softly at first and then louder again as he looked me up and down. He pushed past me without saying anything and started stomping down the breezeway stairs.

"Wait," I said, trying to follow him and nearly falling down the stairs on my twisted ankle. "Where are you going?"

"I'm gonna fucking kill him!" Dad said, a few seconds before his car door slammed and the engine kicked to life. I reached the parking lot just in time to see him speeding off into the night. Layla was already getting out of her car and walking over, her eyes wide.

"What was that?" she said.

"We have to go," I said, limping past her to her car.

"Where's he going?"

"Grant's house," I said, my hands shaking as I buckled myself in.

CHAPTER
THIRTY

The car slipped in the mud as we careened down the canopied dirt road to Grant's trailer. I had my car door open before Layla could even bring the car to a stop. Dad's car was parked ahead, his headlights bathing the front of the trailer ghostly white. He was standing halfway in the driver's seat, his palm pressed on the horn without letting up. The chained-up dogs barked and howled madly trying to attack him, trying to escape, trying to get the noise to stop.

Grant appeared on the porch, his jacket gone and his tie loosened. He squared his shoulders as he strode purposefully down to the yard and over to Dad, who finally let go of the horn. I scrambled to get free of my seat belt and fell down in the mud beside the car.

"Dad!" I yelled. "Dad, please—"

"Go home!" Dad screamed, stepping away from the car

and closing the distance between himself and Grant.

"I don't know what you think," Grant said, raising both of his hands palms out, "but—"

Dad stepped forward, pivoted, and drove his fist into Grant's face with the kind of wild, berserk swing I couldn't have imagined he had in him. Grant made a sound like an airbag exploding and fell back, already bleeding from his nose.

"Listen close, son," Dad growled. "You touch her again, or come near her, or talk to her, or so much as *look* at her, and I *will* put you in the goddamn ground."

I made it to my feet and threw myself between them. Dad looked at me the same way he used to when I was four and I'd thrown a temper tantrum over something stupid, only now his eyes were rimmed red and I saw his nostrils flaring over and over. I heard the screen door slam and turned to see Grant's mom standing on the small porch in a nightgown.

"I'm gonna count to ten," Ruby said, "and then I want you and your faggot son off my property or I call the cops."

"Dad," I said, tugging gently on his sleeve and trying to avoid looking at Grant, "come on."

"One," Grant's mom said.

"Dad," I hissed. He shoved my hand away from his arm.

"Two," she said through gritted teeth. "Three."

"Get in the car," Dad said finally, turning without looking at me. I followed him. Layla waved me down and gave me a wide-eyed look but I shook my head and got in the car with Dad. He jerked the gear stick like he was trying to choke it and pulled out onto the orange-glowing highway.

"It wasn't him," I said after a moment, trying to shrink myself down as small as possible. "It was this other guy—"

"Goddamnit!" Dad said, pounding his other fist against the steering wheel. I pressed myself into the passenger door and stared at him, afraid to speak. "I told you. I *fucking* told you!"

"Dad," I said. "Please. I'm sorry."

"You could've died," he said, his voice still booming in the tiny space, "and you don't even care! Damnit, Amanda—"

"Dad—" I said, my voice cracking.

"Well, I'm done," Dad said. "I'm not watching you destroy yourself. When we get home I want you to pack your things."

NOVEMBER, THREE YEARS AGO

I would have preferred to sit in the back of the bus, but older, meaner boys sat back there, and the assistant principal said I was only making myself a target. Not that sitting up front helped; they kicked at my legs and slapped things out of my hands when they walked by. For a while my shins were striped with green and purple bruises and my paperbacks came home with torn covers and missing pages. Now I sat quietly with my knees pulled to my chest and stared straight ahead.

The bus stopped. I clutched my legs tighter and recognized the thud of Wayne Granville's boots as he walked up the aisle. He stopped at my bench and leaned in, elbows braced on the seat backs. He was a few inches shorter than me but much denser, faster and stronger.

"You have a good Halloween?" he asked. A blonde junior girl rolled her eyes and squeezed past. He didn't seem to notice her. I didn't answer. "Billy says you did. Says he saw you trick-or-treating in a dress." I pressed my forehead into my knees and closed my eyes. I had spent Halloween in my room, alone, doing homework or playing video games. I spent every night and every weekend in my room, alone, playing video games. "Oh, and I heard you blew a buncha dudes for Skittles. Taste the rainbow, right?" The bus driver gave him an impatient look, and Wayne turned to leave. "See you tomorrow, Andy!" he called out as he stepped off the bus.

"No you won't," I whispered, but nobody heard.

The door hissed open at my stop. I shuffled out to the sidewalk and watched the bus leave. The street was empty. The edges of every yard were fortified with black and orange leaf bags, like sandbags with no flood to hold back. I put one foot in front of the other. The wind howled down the street, whipping my hair into my eyes. I let it fall where it wanted; if I wandered into the street and a car hit me, all it would do was save me some time.

Our yard was choked with leaves. Mom had broken her ankle at work a week ago, and most days I could barely manage the effort to get out of bed. My feet broke through the upper layer of new, dry leaves to the dark, mulchy layer beneath. Old rainwater soaked through to my socks, but it didn't matter. I opened the door and entered silently.

Inside, the sound of daytime television drifted out of Mom's room. I put my backpack on the couch and walked softly to her door, peeking in. Her head poked out of the covers while her chest rose and fell slowly. Soft snoring was just barely audible over *Dr Phil*. Two white prescription bottles and a half-empty glass of water sat on the nightstand closest to the door. I took off my shoes and socks and tiptoed over to the nightstand. I picked up the first bottle slowly and read the label: Amoxicillin. I wasn't looking for antibiotics. I set it down and took the other bottle, which I knew now was oxycodone. The bottle rattled as my hands began to shake. Mom mumbled something and I froze. A moment later she turned over and resumed snoring.

I went back to the living room and put the bottle down on the coffee table, then walked to the kitchen where I filled a tall glass with tap water. I sat next to my backpack and put the glass of water next to the pill bottle. I took my *Health & Wellness* textbook out of my backpack and put it in my lap. A running male body with muscles and veins and bones exposed stared out from beneath the title. I ran my hand down the cover and imagined the tendons beneath my skin, the bones they were attached to, the blood running through spiderwebbed veins, the muscles made of a hundred thousand tiny cords. This body, this walking prison, had forced me to keep it alive for fifteen years.

I opened the textbook to the page that read, "*What Boys Can Expect from Puberty*". Then I opened the pill bottle, removed three small white pills, and put them in my mouth. They tasted powdery and bitter. I swallowed them with a sip of water and kept reading. I read the text on the page and felt the things it described happening to my own body – I was a late bloomer at fifteen, tall but beardless and scrawny, with a high voice that still squeaked sometimes, but I could feel the changes coming like a swarm of insects skittering across my bones.

Testes will descend from the body and begin producing testosterone and sperm.

I swallowed three more pills. I wouldn't be a friendless victim any more.

Spontaneous erections and nocturnal emissions are normal and should not be cause for alarm.

I swallowed three more pills. No more caring that Dad didn't care about me.

Thick, coarse hair will appear on the face, chest and stomach, with leg and arm hair noticeably thicker than females.

I swallowed three more pills. My limbs felt heavy and strange. No more future with no love, no kisses, no closeness.

The voice will drop by about an octave as the larynx enlarges and hardens.

I swallowed three more pills. It was difficult to focus. No more possibility of shaming Mom with the knowledge of the kind of life I actually wanted.

Bone density and muscle mass increase and shoulders widen disproportionately, giving males and females distinct skeletal shapes.

I swallowed three more pills. I was very sleepy. Everything felt okay though. I knew everything would be okay. The bottom of the page said something about acne and body odour but the words danced whenever I tried to move my eyes over them. I closed the book and set it aside. I took the remaining pills and the glass of water and moved to the bathroom. I removed my clothes and sat down in the tub because I didn't want to leave a mess. Leaving a mess would have been rude. I realized that I forgot to write a note but it was too late for that now, and soon nothing would matter at all. My eyes slid shut.

Everything was going to be okay.

CHAPTER
THIRTY-ONE

The bus smelled of body odour and dry heating-vent air and urine. It was just after noon when we left; Dad had at least let me sleep in and fed me breakfast in silence. The man in the aisle seat was snoring loudly, but I didn't care. I wanted to sleep, was tired enough to sleep, but couldn't. I felt dead inside. I felt nothing.

I tried putting headphones in but by the time we reached Chattanooga and switched from I-24 to I-75, I had tried all my favourite songs and they all sounded like musical styrofoam. I read articles on the internet but they were all trivial. I wanted to be home, but I didn't know what home was any more. I pressed my cheek to the glass, the road slipping by like a black ribbon thrown across the hills. I watched the changing scenery of this place where I was born that had been telling me it hated me for as long as I could remember and gave in to the static behind my eyes.

* * *

The jolt of the bus coming to a stop sent me sitting straight up with a sharp breath. I shuffled down the aisle and descended the stairs. I stood for a moment in the fumes and noise of the Greyhound station, still feeling numb and cold.

"Yoo-hoo!" a loud female voice called, high and musical. It took me a moment to realize it was Mom. I looked in her direction and froze when I saw her sitting next to Virginia, both of them waving, Mom in a zip-up purple windbreaker and sneakers, and Virginia in an oversize cable-knit sweater that came to her knees. My head swam, watching them together.

"Hi," I said, putting my bags down and hugging each of them before giving them a confused look. "So, this is weird."

"Is it?" Mom said, giving Virginia a look of concern.

"I don't think so," Virginia said, taking my bag for me as we made our way out to the sidewalk where Mom was parked.

"But you two barely know each other."

"Don't we?" Virginia said, smiling mischievously.

"I started going to that support group at your therapist's office," Mom explained as we got in her old grey SUV. I tried to picture Mom at the meetings and couldn't. Mom must have known what I was thinking because she shrugged and said, "I got lonely and I wanted to know more about you, so I decided to check it out." She squeezed my leg and gave me a look that told me everything was going to be okay. I put my hand over hers and smiled, silently thanking her for not mentioning that I had left town with a black eye and came back with one too.

The house was even cleaner than I remembered, and decked out in decorations for Thanksgiving, which was still a few days away. The living room and kitchen were explosions of orange and brown, with paper turkeys and cornucopias on every surface with any room. I smelled a roast in the oven, and spicy cornbread, and my mouth watered.

"That smells so good," I said. "You didn't have to go to the trouble."

"You're my daughter!" Mom said. "And you're too skinny. I knew your daddy couldn't even be trusted to feed you." She walked into the kitchen and announced that dinner was in half an hour.

"I need some fresh air after the bus," I yelled back.

"I'll join you," Virginia said, stepping outside with me.

"You staying for Thanksgiving?" I said as she put on her jacket.

"Wish I could," she said, fiddling with her buttons as she descended the porch steps. "I'm actually moving down to Savannah next week. Got accepted to SCAD."

"That's so cool!" I said. She beamed at me and we

walked in silence for a moment. I winced with each step. My ankle still throbbed. "So," I said eventually, "you wanna know what happened?"

"Let's talk about something else," Virginia said. "Give you a little time. You deleted your Tumblr, didn't you?" I nodded. "So you still don't know what everybody's been up to." I shook my head, glad she was talking. Virginia and Mom were the only two people who could have been around me right now.

"Zeke finally got a job with insurance that covers his top surgery," she said. "You just missed the party; he's got the surgery scheduled for next month."

"That's great. Is he still dating Rhonda?"

"Moira's couch-surfing again," Virginia said suddenly, as if she hadn't heard me. "She's stayed clean so far, but she's a long way from safe. Your mom's thinking of putting her up in y'all's guest room." She put her hands in her pockets and looked up at the sheet of iron-grey clouds overhead. "Your mom's a really great person, you know."

"I know," I said, tilting my head and narrowing my eyes. "Virginia. What happened to Rhonda?"

"Can I tell you later?" Virginia asked, giving me a pleading look. "You're under enough stress as it is."

"I'd like to know," I said.

"Okay." She took a deep breath and closed her eyes. "She killed herself about a month ago, just after I got back. Didn't leave a note."

"No," I said, covering my mouth and wrapping my other arm around myself. "Jesus. Why?"

"You know why," Virginia said, shaking her head slowly. "We all know why." She was silent for a moment while I processed that information. "Her parents were monsters about the whole thing, of course. They lopped all her hair off and buried her in a suit and tie."

We walked in silence for a while, lost in our thoughts. Rhonda wasn't the first friend I'd lost; since joining group, I'd been on the other end of that middle-of-the-night phone call too many times. I used to wonder if someone would ever have to make one of those calls for me.

"So what's next?" Virginia asked after a while, as we headed back towards home.

"I don't know," I said, letting the wind whip my hair into my eyes as I put one foot achingly in front of the other. "This time, I really don't know."

CHAPTER
THIRTY-TWO

For most of my life Thanksgiving had been a huge, noisy day full of grandparents, great-aunts and -uncles, cousins, half cousins and nieces, but ever since coming out and living as a girl full-time, Mom and I had been informally exiled from all family functions. That was fine by me; I much preferred the kind of quiet, cosy meal I was sharing with Mom the Thanksgiving after I came back home.

She had made too much food like she always did. We were going to be eating leftovers for weeks. We mostly ate in silence, which could have been awkward but was somehow comforting. Mom knew I wasn't ready to talk about what had happened and I loved her for giving me the space. Halfway through dinner I heard a scratch at the door.

"Could you let the cat in?" Mom said.

I opened the front door and the cat trotted through, giving me three loud, terse meows to register her complaint at having been made to wait. The cold, wet air was bracing after the drowsy heat inside. I stepped out to the porch and leaned against the rail with my eyes closed for just a moment, enjoying the chill. My eyes snapped open again when I heard the sound of tyres crunching down the driveway. I recognized Dad's car immediately. I didn't say anything as he stepped out of the car with a covered casserole dish under his arm.

When he neared the porch I smelled his sweet-potato casserole with the marshmallow crust on top.

"Hi," he said, looking rickety and out of place. He tried to smile and, despite everything in the last few weeks, I couldn't resist smiling back at him. "Am I late?"

"What are you doing here?" I asked instead. He stopped just inside the door and looked around quietly, like our living room was a strange foreign country.

"Amanda?" Mom called from the other room. Her chair squeaked and I heard her feet coming from around the corner. "Is someone – oh." She froze when she rounded the corner. Dad finished taking off his coat and waved sheepishly.

"Happy Thanksgiving," he said. I leaned against the back of the couch and looked back and forth between them, waiting for the detonation. I had always wondered what would happen if they ever saw each other in person again, and the most likely outcome seemed to be a full thermonuclear exchange. Instead, Dad said, "Your home is lovely," and Mom replied, "Thank you. Come join us."

The conversation didn't improve much after Dad arrived, but that was okay. We finished the meal in silence and Mom started to clear away the dishes. Dad got up to help but I touched his forearm to get his attention.

"Actually," I said, "could we go for a walk? Rain's been gone for a few hours."

"Yeah?" Dad said.

"I just thought," I said, "there's a baseball diamond they keep lit at night." Dad stood there, holding a stack of plates, blinking slowly. "We could, you know, play catch…if you still want to."

"Oh," Dad said. He put the plates down and thought for a moment. "You're sure?"

"I'm sure," I said.

"I'd like that," Dad said.

Mom was more than happy to keep us out of the kitchen, since she had her own arcane way of loading the dishwasher that nobody could ever get quite right. The gloves and ball were in an old box, unused and dusty after more than a decade. The squelching and slipping as our boots worked their way through the wet leaves and muck made me glad my ankle had almost completely healed. Dad was silent for the entire walk, staring from the sky to me and back again.

"Something on your mind?" he said.

"A lot."

"That's understandable." Dad shoved his hands in his pockets and stared up at the street lamps.

We arrived at the baseball diamond, the mist making the light from the floodlights weak and pale. He stood where the batter would stand and I stood on the pitcher's mound, mitt on my left hand and ball in my right.

"Why do I have to wear the mitt on my left hand?" I said. "Wouldn't it be easier to catch with my right?"

"Sure," Dad said, "but can you throw with your left?"

"Oh," I said, nodding. I hauled back, cocked my arm, and threw the baseball to him as hard as I could. It sailed over him and to the left, clanking into the chain-link fence protecting the bleachers. "Oops! Sorry."

I saw him smiling as he jogged back into position and couldn't help laughing.

"What's so funny?" he said, tossing the ball in the air absent-mindedly.

"Nothing," I said. "It's just sometimes I wonder what my past self would think if she saw me, and I wondered what our past selves would think if they saw us right now." He thought about it for a moment, his smile widening more and more, until we both snorted and the laughter popped out of us. We carried on like that for a little while, him throwing, me failing to catch, me throwing so wildly that he had to duck out of the way or run halfway across the field to retrieve the ball.

"So when your mother and me talked before you came to live with me," Dad said, finally breaking the silence, "she told me your therapist said you were real fragile after what happened last summer, at the mall. I wouldn't—" he started and faltered. "If anything like that ever happened now…"

"Oh," I said, shrugging. "I think maybe I'm stronger than that now."

Dad nodded, the relief plain on his face. "I think maybe you're right."

"Yeah?"

"The girl who moved in with me wouldn't have been okay after that homecoming dust-up." I nodded, thinking of the shocked faces of my classmates in the dim light of the gymnasium, the twisting in my gut when Grant said *It's not true, right?*, the horror of racing away from Parker in the darkened woods. "Dust-up" seemed like an understatement.

"I guess not," I said.

"I've just been thinking," Dad said. "You know I went in the navy after high school, don't you?" I nodded and threw the ball so it rolled between his legs. "I thought I was tough. A lot of guys thought they were even tougher." He threw the ball. I yelped, closed my eyes, and by some miracle actually caught it. "I don't think we held a candle to you."

275

"I'm not brave," I said, smiling despite myself. "Bravery implies I had a choice. I'm just me, you know?" I threw the ball into the palm of my glove over and over while I spoke, staring at the floodlight until blotches danced in my eyes. I had sent my application in to NYU, and in a few months I would find out whether I got in or not. I imagined falling off the face of the earth again, drifting out of Layla, Anna and Chloe's lives, being mostly forgotten by my classmates except as an occasional story trotted out at parties. Grant was gone, which hurt but was also kind of a relief – he was one less complication when it came time to pack my things and head up north. Everything about that plan was fine except for one thing: I didn't want to disappear any more.

I looked up at my father. "What if I told you I wanted to go back to Lambertville?" I saw him staring at me. Was his face white from the chill, or from fear? "Would that be a brave thing to do, or would it be stupid?"

"Both?" Dad said, running a hand over his moist hair and blowing out a long breath. "But that's what being young is, really. I think I've been so afraid for you all this time that I forgot that."

"Since I moved in, you mean?" I said, throwing the ball so that he only had to jump a little bit to catch it.

"Oh no," he said, "longer than that. Since you were just a baby."

"I thought you were embarrassed by me."

"I was," he said, chewing his lip. "I pray the Lord forgives

276

me one day but I was. More than that, though, so much more than that, I was terrified for you." I looked down and flexed my glove. "I had to drink just to let your mother teach you how to walk; I kept seeing visions of you falling and cracking your head open."

"I think I get that from you," I said, smiling. He chuckled darkly.

"I couldn't stand the idea of you hurting. I couldn't stand the idea of anything taking away your happiness." He shrugged and sighed. "But everything that made you happy, from the way you wanted to walk to the toys you wanted to the way you wanted to dress…it put you in danger. So what could I do?"

"You ran away," I said.

"I ran away." He walked over to me, taking his glove off and slipping it under his armpit. "Or I let you run away and chose not to follow. Either way…" He put his hands on my shoulders and looked me straight in the eye. "You *are* brave," he said. "You get *that* from your mother." He removed his hands and stared off at the dark, empty park. "After homecoming, when you walked in that door – I was furious. So mad I felt like I could kill someone. Mad at you, mad at myself, mad at whoever had done that to you. But then when you were gone and I was all alone in that apartment, thinking about everything you went through…I wanted another chance to get it right." He took a deep breath and looked back at me. "I guess what

I'm trying to say is, if you want to come back to Lambertville, well, I'd be real happy to have my daughter back."

I nodded, a lump in my throat. I had been waiting my whole life for my father to want me, for him to want his daughter. I blinked back tears, but this time, they were tears of joy.

We walked back to the house, a different kind of silence falling between us. I caught his eye and he put his arm around my shoulder, pulling me in close. When we got to the house he opened the trash-can lid and tossed the baseball mitts inside.

"Bye, Andrew," I said softly.

"Bye, son," Dad agreed, as we went inside.

APRIL, TWO YEARS AGO

"Hardy?" the nurse said. "Andrew Hardy?"

I stood and took a few steps towards the door. The horrible twisting in my gut that normally accompanied the sound of that name was barely present. I was too excited about what was about to happen.

"Andr— Amanda?" Mom said. I turned and saw her standing with her hands clasped, a look on her face like she was afraid this was the last time she would ever see me. "Do you want me to come with you?"

"No, thank you," I said. I hugged her and backed away again. "I think I need to do this by myself."

I turned back to the nurse and followed her into a bright, white hallway. She had me stand on a scale and clucked reproachfully when she saw how underweight I was. Then she had me sit on the paper-covered examination bed and took my blood pressure, which was normal, and asked me the usual questions. Did I have any allergies? No. What medications was I taking? Wellbutrin and Lexapro. Did I have any ongoing medical problems? Not really.

"So what brings you to us today?" the nurse said finally.

"My therapist referred me," I said, my voice barely above a whisper. I hesitated in saying the rest. "I have, um, gender identity disorder. I'm…I'm transgender." I tore absent-mindedly at the paper seat cover and took a deep breath. "I need to start hormones."

"Okie dokie," the nurse said, scribbling one last note before smiling and closing my file. "You just sit tight and Dr Howard will be with you shortly."

I fell back on the bed, stared at the ceiling, and crossed my hands over my heart. It was really happening. It was really, finally happening. I wasn't going to grow hair on my chest and back. My voice wasn't going to deepen any more than the little bit it already had. My shoulders weren't going to widen. My jaw and forehead weren't going to bulge. I was never going to grow a beard. All because of this moment. I heard the door open and sat up to see an older man with a thick beard and bald head examining my chart.

"Afternoon, Andrew," he said, putting down the chart and holding out his hand. I shook it and he smiled. "I'm Dr Howard. How are you doing today?"

"Good," I said, and I felt a sudden, unprecedented surge of courage, "but I would prefer it if you called me Amanda, sir."

"I see," Dr Howard said, still smiling. "No problem, Amanda. Let me just make a note of that in your chart." He made the note quickly. "Let them know at the desk if anyone gives you any problems about that in the future."

"Thank you, sir."

"I've looked at your chart and gone through the notes your therapist sent us," Dr Howard said, "and this all seems pretty straightforward. We'll start you on one hundred milligrams of spironolactone to block your testosterone and two milligrams of estradiol to replace it with oestrogen. We're starting at a low dose at first because you're going to have some mood instability and the estradiol can be hard on your liver. I like to ease in so we can observe you and make sure things don't get out of hand. We'll bring you in for a blood test in about a month and stay in touch with your therapist and see how we want to proceed from there."

"Yes, sir," I said.

"There is one other thing I want to go over before I write this prescription though," he said. "Your therapist doesn't seem to have any doubts, and I don't doubt his skill at his job, but I would be remiss if I didn't make sure you understand a few things."

"Okay," I said, my throat feeling suddenly dry. I was so close, and some small, scared part of me screamed that he was about to take it all away.

"Not to be crude, but you are going to grow breasts,"

Dr Howard continued. "They'll shrink if you ever change your mind and go off the hormones, but they'll never completely go away unless you get reconstructive surgery." I nodded. "And more importantly, you're going to be sterile within a few weeks of starting the spironolactone. It *might* be reversible if you stop the hormones within your first year, but after that point the effect is almost completely permanent."

"I understand," I said, looking down at my hands.

"All right then," he said, pulling out a prescription pad and scribbling on it. "Stop by the front desk to take care of your payment and make your next appointment, and I'll see you back here in a month. Good to meet you, Amanda."

"You too," I said, feeling like I was walking through a dream as I made my way back to the lobby.

Later that night, after the moon had risen and Mom had long since gone to sleep, I took my bottle of estradiol and a can of Diet Coke into the backyard. The grass was cool and wet between my toes, and the frogs and crickets were singing softer than usual. I fell back in the grass and stared up at the faintly glowing crescent moon. Its points were facing to the right, which meant it was just emerging from the darkness of the new moon.

I opened the pill bottle, fished one out, and held it above me. The tiny blue oval felt dry and powdery on my wet fingers. God, it was so small, only a third the size of my pinky nail, and yet it was everything. Breasts and sterility were irreversible side effects, but I knew I was never going back.

It was going to be hard. I was going to have to pretend to be a boy for a little while longer. No matter how much I tried to hide it, classmates and family members were going to notice my body change. The bullying would probably be worse than ever, but somehow, now, I felt like I could handle it. I felt like, as Amanda, I could face things that would have kept me cowering in bed before.

I closed my eyes, placed the pill on my tongue, and washed it down with a sweet, bubbling sip of soda. Then I lay my head back down, closed my eyes, and bathed in moonlight, letting myself dream of how good life could be every now and then.

CHAPTER
THIRTY-THREE

The girls picked me up outside Dad's apartment for the first day of my second semester in Lambertville. I settled into the left rear seat, next to Chloe, same as always, and in the quiet moment before we would hurriedly catch up with one another I breathed and marvelled at how normal everything felt. The world had ended, and yet the world was still here.

"The prodigal daughter returns!" Layla said, beaming at me in the rear-view.

"It's good to be back," I told them honestly. "I missed you guys." I hesitated for a moment, then asked what I'd been afraid to ask. I leaned forward so my head was between the two front seats and looked at Anna. I couldn't help noticing she was having a hard time looking at me. "Are we okay?"

Anna started to say something, but Layla gave her a

dangerous look. She looked thoughtful, and started again. "Lord knows I don't walk the straight and narrow," she said, very primly. "None of us is perfect except God, right? So I think it's a sin –" there was another furious look from Layla –"but I think *lots* of things are sins and Jesus died so we'd be forgiven for our sins, so…"

"Okay," I said, gently putting a hand on her shoulder, "but are you still my *friend*?"

"Of course!" Anna said. "Just 'cause I'm grappling with the…the…"

"The metaphysics," Layla said.

"With the metaphysics doesn't mean I don't still love you and Chloe like sisters!"

"That's all I need to know then," I said, falling back into my seat and sharing a smile with Chloe.

"I did do some reading though, online," Anna said, turning to face me. "And if I ever do or say anything homophobic or transphobic, y'all just let me know, okay? And I'll have a talk with the folks at church, Amanda, 'cause everybody loved you and I want you to feel comfortable coming back."

I put my hand over hers and felt a prickling tenderness in my fingertips. "Thank you."

"Of course she's the one that gets thanked," Layla said. "You and Chloe with your super-secret queer girls club—"

"Actually," Chloe said, stifling a laugh and glancing at me, "I had no idea she was tra—"

"And Anna just mutters something about Jesus sort of loving you and suddenly she's an angel and meanwhile I was *there with you* when your dad punched Grant—"

"Your dad punched Grant?" Anna said, her mouth wide.

"I pulled a loaded gun on Parker," Chloe reminded nobody in particular.

"But who cares about Layla? No one, obviously! I'm just the girl with the car nobody gives a shit about, so why—"

"Layla!" I said. She stopped and glanced back at me. I hugged her from behind and kissed the top of her head. "*You* shush. You're a treasure. Thank you guys so much." I thought of Andrew then, that sad child who wanted desperately for someone to be a friend, for someone to understand, who never could have imagined a future like this. Who couldn't imagine a future at all.

"That's all I wanted," Layla said, flipping her hair and giving a haughty look to the middle distance as she pulled into the parking lot. "Just, you know, some recognition of my grandeur."

We all got out of the car and hugged. Anna and Layla had to rush off to an early student-government meeting, but Chloe and I had nowhere in particular to be for fifteen minutes.

"I wanted to say I'm sorry," Chloe said as we sat cross-legged in the grass by the front steps. "For being jealous about Bee. I know you never liked her like that."

I sighed. "No, not like that," I said. "But I'm still sorry." I hadn't heard from Bee yet, and I wasn't sure what it would be like when I saw her. Maybe she would try to apologize, try to be my friend again. But no matter what she said, I knew I couldn't let her back into my life. What she did hurt me even more than Parker, even more than the assault in the mall bathroom, because I had trusted her. I knew now I would have to be careful with who I let myself get close to. But maybe that was a lesson everybody had to learn.

"Don't apologize," Chloe said. She plucked two long pieces of grass and held them between her index and middle fingers. "Really, don't. It was just that you were new, and pretty, and you just came in and got everything you wanted, and then it felt like you took her too. And it was like everything was so hard for me, while it seemed so easy for you. But I know now that it ain't that simple."

I gave her a wry smile. "No. 'Simple' is not a word that has ever described my life."

We sat for a few minutes in pleasant silence before I asked, "So I haven't heard anything since homecoming… how's your family been about the news?"

"My folks're a work in progress," Chloe said with a shrug. "My brothers sort of always knew, and they're more or less okay. They say Bee's lucky she's a girl or they'd've run her over in our pickup for what she did at homecoming."

"Misogyny saves the day?" I said.

"It's all bluster," Chloe said, letting the blades of grass get blown away by the wind.

"Chloe?" I said, looking around to make sure nobody was looking. "I'm going to do something now, as a friend, okay?"

"Okay," she said, knitting her brows. I pulled her into a bone-crushing hug and kissed her on the cheek. "You are a fucking *amazing* girl and whatever town you end up in, whatever girl you end up with, they're all lucky to have you."

"Thank you," Chloe said, her cheeks bright red. She brushed off her jeans as we both stood up. "And you – whatever guy you end up with'll be lucky too." She slung her backpack over her shoulder. "Think it'll be Grant? Is there any way?"

I checked the clock on my phone, stood, and shrugged as I picked up my own bag. "I have no idea," I said. "But I guess I'll find out today."

As I made my way to homeroom, I kept my eyes locked on the glossy floor tiles, afraid to look up and make eye contact with my classmates. The bell hadn't rung yet and the hallways reverberated with the sounds of sneakers on floor tile and slamming locker doors.

"Welcome back," I heard a voice say, and looked up to see a mousy girl with cat-eye glasses gripping the straps of her backpack and smiling at me. She looked vaguely familiar, but I didn't think we'd ever spoken before. I realized that even though I didn't know her, she knew me, and the thought that she noticed I was gone – and that I'd come back – made me smile.

I continued down the hall with my head held high. A few classmates looked away when I passed, but the rest nodded in my direction or waved. As I rounded the corner towards homeroom, I stopped short. A dozen students were milling outside the locked classroom door, waiting for the teacher to arrive, and my eyes were immediately drawn to Grant's broad back. My mouth tugged in a smile at the sight of him, but then he turned around, and my brain caught up.

The crowd parted for him easily, all eyes on us. He looked around and registered how many people were staring. "Can we go somewhere else?"

I nodded and together we walked down the hall and into the empty cafeteria.

When the doors closed behind us he looked up. His eyes were shining, his gaze unreadable.

"Hey," he said again.

"Hey." I looked down. "How are you?"

"I got news," he said, squinting and rubbing the back of his neck, looking away again. "I won the Hope Scholarship to go down to Chatt State."

"Congratulations!" I said, meaning it. "I'm really happy

for you." Our eyes met again for a moment and words passed silently between us. *I love you* and *I need you. I'm sorry* and *forgive me.*

"Sorry about my dad," I said finally.

"Ah," he said, rubbing the bridge of his nose where the blow had hit. "He's got a *mean* right hook for an old guy."

I looked away, but couldn't help smiling. "I'll tell him you said so."

"I understand though," Grant said. I returned my eyes to him. He was leaning against the wall, looking up at the lights, picking nervously at his thumbnail. "What Parker did...your dad thought it was me." I nodded. "It's not exactly the same, but if anybody hurt Avery or Harper..." He clenched his fists. His eyes were wide when they met mine again, and there was too much behind them to decipher. "I'd probably do more than punch 'em."

"I'm glad you understand," I said, reaching out to touch his arm but stopping myself. He noticed the movement and sighed.

The bell rang, but neither of us moved.

"You didn't call," I said, trying to keep the hurt from my voice.

"Neither did you," Grant said softly before giving me a rueful smile.

"I guess not," I said, running my fingers through my hair. "I assumed you were done with me." I looked up, taking in his long-lashed dark eyes and boyish, open face.

I thought about the first time we kissed, the feeling of weightlessness at the lake, driving in his truck, all the moments we had shared, and the memories he had given me. They were the realest, truest moments of my life, and yet to him, they now probably felt like lies. "Honestly, I would have understood if you were done with me."

"Yeah?"

"I never wanted you to find out that way," I told him. "I'm sorry if I…embarrassed you." For a second I found the old shame creeping up, threatening to pull me back under.

"More embarrassing for you," he said. I took a deep breath and closed my eyes.

"I told you I loved you at the dance," I said. "I didn't know if you'd heard me."

He shook his head. My heart throbbed.

"I didn't abandon Tommy," he said, his expression serious, "and I won't abandon you."

I exhaled a breath. "That's sweet, but what does that *mean*?" I shook my head. "Do you love me?"

"Yes."

"You do?" I said, taken aback.

"I've shared more of myself with you than anybody else," he said. "And, even if I burned the note, you shared everything with me. Whatever we are…"

"'Whatever we are'?" I said, my throat clenching up. "So we're not…?"

"I don't know," he said. "I tried to look stuff up while

you were gone, but I don't have a computer, and it turns out when you do a search for 'transsexual' on the library computers – let's just say I ain't allowed in the library for a while." He rubbed his arm and opened his mouth a few times, trying to find the right words. "I don't know if I can understand, and even if I can understand I just don't know…" He trailed off. His shoulders sagged. "I don't know, Amanda. I just…I just wish you were a girl." His eyes widened as the words came out. "I mean, I wish you were never…I wish you were always…"

"No," I said, the strength in my voice surprising me, that one word so clear in the empty space. He sniffed and shifted his weight. "I was *always* a girl, *always*," I said, my eyes burning. "See you around, Grant." I turned and started to walk away but he grabbed my shoulder.

"I wanna try," he said. He took his hand away and I turned back. "I think I need to hear it from you, though."

I heard the kids down the hall shuffling into homeroom. I stayed where I was. "I still have the letter I wrote you," I said slowly. "I could print it again."

"No," he said. "I'd like you to tell me face-to-face."

"Okay," I said after a moment. "How about tonight?"

Grant's car motor was the only sound cutting the peaceful silence of the lake. I turned and watched him get out, my heart hammering at my chest. In the soft light at the end of the day, it felt like I was seeing him for the first time. His shaggy black hair rippled in the soft, cold breeze, and his dark eyes practically twinkled when they caught mine. He was wearing a faded old hoodie, jeans and work boots, but even through his clothes I could tell how strong and graceful he was when he walked.

"Evening," he said, flashing me a smile.

"Hi," I said, taking a long, deep breath and closing my eyes. A silent moment passed as I readied myself for what was to come. "Where do you want me to start?"

"At the beginning," Grant said. In the distance, a lone cicada made its call. "I wanna know everything, if you're okay with telling me."

"Okay," I said, as I led him to the tree house. We settled in, not looking at each other, our eyes trained ahead on the sparkling water as it faded from the brightness of day to the dark glimmer of night. "I'll start with my birth name."

As I spoke I thought back to what Virginia had said weeks before, about getting anything you wanted if you let yourself believe you deserved it. For as long as I could remember, I had been apologizing for existing, for trying to be who I was, to live the life I was meant to lead. Maybe this would be the last conversation I would ever have with Grant. Maybe not. Either way, I realized, I wasn't sorry I existed any more. I deserved to live. I deserved to find love. I knew now – I believed, now – that I deserved to be loved.

*Read on for a note to readers
from author Meredith Russo...*

A NOTE FROM THE AUTHOR

To my cisgender readers – which is to say, to those of you who are not trans: Thank you for reading this. Thank you for being interested. I'm nervous about what you might think of this book, though maybe not in the way you might think. I am, of course, anxious that people might not like it, but even more than that I'm worried that you might take Amanda's story as gospel, especially since it comes from a trans woman. This prospect terrifies me, actually! I am a storyteller, not an educator. I have taken liberties with what I know reality to be. I have fictionalized things to make them work in my story. I have, in some ways, cleaved to stereotypes and even bent rules to make Amanda's trans-ness as unchallenging to normative assumptions as possible. She knew from a very young age. She is exclusively attracted to boys. She is entirely feminine. She passes as a woman with little to no effort. She had surgery that her family should not have been able to afford, and she started hormones through legitimate channels before she probably could have in the real world. I did this because I wanted you to have no possible barrier to understanding Amanda as a teenage girl with a different medical history from most other girls. Amanda's life and identity would be just as valid if she didn't figure herself out until later in life, or if she were a tomboy, or if she were bisexual or a lesbian or asexual, or if she had trouble passing, or if she either could not or chose not to get "bottom" surgery. Grant's attraction to her in any of these scenarios would have been no less heterosexual, nor would Bee's have been any less homosexual. It is easy to get hung up on these points if you haven't lived our lives though, so I wanted to set those aside. I hope that, having got to know Amanda, you will not apply the details of her experience as dogma other trans people must adhere to but rather as inspiration to pursue an ever broader understanding of our lives and identities, as well as your own understanding of gender and sex.

To my trans readers: It's okay if you're different from Amanda. She isn't real, and you are. I spent the better part of two decades trying to convince myself that I wasn't something I knew myself to be because I didn't fit a very specific, very toxic model of what society says transgender people are, and trust me when I say that my life story is radically different from Amanda's. It's okay to be trans and also gay, lesbian, bisexual, asexual, or anything else. It's okay to be trans and not pass (and you can still be legitimately *beautiful* without passing), and it's okay to be trans and pass and go completely stealth. It's okay to be a trans man. It's okay to be genderqueer, or to change identities more than once in your life, or to feel you have no gender at all. It's okay to be trans and never pursue any of the medical aspects of transitioning, and it's also okay to be trans and alter your body in whatever ways you want. There is no wrong way to express and embody your most authentic self! You are beautiful, and you deserve to have your body and identity and agency respected.

I know it hurts. I know it hurts so bad you can barely breathe sometimes. I know because I've been there. Please don't leave us. I promise life can be good, and we need you too much.

IF YOU HAVE BEEN AFFECTED
BY THE ISSUES RAISED IN THIS BOOK,
THE FOLLOWING ORGANISATIONS
CAN HELP.

Samaritans are available round the clock,
every single day of the year.

Talk to us any time you like in your own way and
off the record, about whatever's getting to you.

Call us free any time on 116 123
Or email jo@samaritans.org
Visit us: find your nearest branch on
samaritans.org

**Family and individual support for teenagers and
children with gender identity issues**
Please reply to: BM Mermaids, London, WC1N 3XX

Mermaids supports children and young people
up to 19 years old suffering from gender
identity issues, and their families and supporting
professionals. Our resources provide a vital lifeline
for young people and families who are searching
for support and information.

www.mermaidsuk.org.uk

Helpline:
0844 334 0550 (landline)*

*Calls to 0844 numbers are charged at 7ppm,
plus the charge from your call provider.*

0344 334 0550 (mobile)

ACKNOWLEDGEMENTS

For teaching me to love a pluralistic world, for encouraging me to fearlessly express myself, and for accepting me as their daughter, I want to thank my parents, Toby and Karol Stroud. Thanks, too, to my sister Katie, who has always had my back, loved me unconditionally, and is *the* force that keeps my head on my shoulders. I've been blessed with an incredible extended family – thanks to all of you as well, for accepting me when I came out, and for the parts all of you played in getting me here. I also want to thank my children, without whom I never would have had the ambition to try something this difficult. And, finally, there is someone whose influence was integral to the soul inside of this story, and without whose prodding this book never would have been finished: Juniper Russo. Thank you.

Thank you to Joelle Hobeika, for ushering me into this crazy job when I was at one of the lowest points in my life, and for seeing the value of this project when I originally proposed it. Thank you to Sara Shandler, who killed more of my darlings than I could have stomached on my own, and without whom this book would have been a sloppy, self-indulgent affair. And then there's Josh Bank, who kept us on target, made everything happen, and pushed for that one killer scene (you know the one). The three of you also deserve huge thanks for taking my coming out as gracefully as you did. I also want to thank Sarah Dotts Barley, Amy Einhorn, and the rest of the team at Flatiron Books for seeing the value of a story about a trans girl written by a trans woman, and for listening to my suggestion that we keep trans people involved at every available step. And, speaking of further trans involvement, I also want to thank the *absolutely* gorgeous cover model of the US edition, Kira Conley, for her participation and belief in this project.

And, finally, thank you to the following individuals, without whose faith and support I might not have survived 2015: Miranda Stroud, Ailish Holmes, Matt and Heather Durham, Aria Taibi, Sam Hightower, Kay Popper, Brooks and Jackie Benjamin, John Burke, Beth Kasner, Bridget DuPey, Laura and Lee Palmiero, Ruby Bolton-Murray, February Keeney, Rachel Goodman, and Becca Reeves. You are, all of you, angels.

ABOUT
MEREDITH RUSSO

MEREDITH RUSSO was born, raised and lives in Tennessee. She started living as her true self in late 2013 and never looked back. *If I Was Your Girl* was partially inspired by her experiences as a trans woman.

When Meredith is not busy writing she can be found reblogging pictures of cats and babies, reading fan fiction and fantasy novels, arguing with strangers about social justice, and raising her two amazing children, Vivian and Darwin.

Like Amanda, Meredith is also a gigantic nerd who spends a lot of her time obsessing over video games and *Star Wars*. *If I Was Your Girl* is her debut novel.